THE DARKEST HOUR

SIR PATRICK BIJOU

PRELUDE

Kate's leap across the pond to an unassuming American town was more than a chance encounter—it was destiny's quiet whisper and the beginning of the most harrowing yet worthwhile adventure of her life.

Drawn by an inexplicable force, Kate is captivated by the enigmatic Ian. Their connection is magnetic but conceals a shadowy truth that lingers beneath the surface.

As their relationship deepens, Kate's world unravels as Ian's haunting secret unfolds before her eyes—a secret that transforms everything she thought she knew about the sleepy town. A chilling realisation unfolds: Ian and his family are more than mere inhabitants. They are guardians of a hidden realm where unearthly forces lurk in the shadows.

With the discovery of Ian's nature, Kate is thrust into an unknown and perilous world. She must navigate through treacherous secrets and sinister entities to keep him in her life. Amidst the darkness that engulfs the town, Kate and Ian must find the strength to survive and stay together, for unravelling these mysteries might cost them more than they ever imagined.

__The Darkest Hour__" is a mesmerising tale of love, danger, sex, and the eerie secrets that cloak a seemingly ordinary town. Gripping and suspenseful, this spellbinding novel will keep you on the edge of your seat until the very last page.

ABOUT THE AUTHOR

Sir Patrick Bijou lives and writes from the United Kingdom and is the author of several books on finance and fiction. He is known for his extraordinary skills in settling and negotiating peace settlements and international law and is a prodigious legal and political adviser. His diverse writing ability has been influenced by many experiences, making him the success he is today.

Sir Patrick has written books and articles about the liberation of people, highlighting the issues of those whom the literary world of creative writing has not enlightened. His expedition into content writing has made him a remarkably inspired author and professional communicator.

He has written over 45 non-fictional and fictional books spanning different genres.

Finding his Books.
To find out more about Sir Patrick, visit his website.

www.sirpatrickbijou.com
www.bijouebook.com

Table of Contents

Chapter 1

Life can be so rude. Snatch us from the known and familiar and, without preface, hurl us into a place that isn't any of those things. Like an unsuspecting pet shop mouse being plucked from the only home it's known, taken away to be pampered, spoiled, and treated like a King of Mice... or fed to a snake.

I was that mouse.

I was growing bored with this town, the same faces, and the same conversations. Perhaps it was time to move on, to continue searching...for what, the meaning of my life? It remained out of my reach, beyond my field of vision, and I sank into an inescapable funk.

I had planned a two-week vacation to England to visit with family and catch up with friends, but my car died, leaving me with a massive repair bill and two weeks of nothing but time. Could I mope around for that long? Hmm, I think I could. I was already off to a good start.

Moping or not, I could not stay in and listen to my roommate's chatter - I showered, dressed in my favorite shredded jeans and silk top, and bunched my hair on my head with a clip. A little makeup and... I couldn't be bothered. I flopped on my bed and watched the ceiling fan's wobbly rotations.

My phone rang. I reached for it without breaking my stare. "Hello?"

"Hey." A long draw and stunted cough " Whacha doin'?" It was my cute, stoner neighbor.

I'm actually staring at a fan, pitiful. "...I'm just heading out".

"Come by later?"

I wasn't interested. "Yeah, maybe...see ya later."

This just wouldn't do. I had to get out. I grabbed some music and headed for our 'Cheers' where everybody knows your name and other details.

I was greeted at the door by our bouncer come cover charge collector. I never saw the need for either here.

"Hey" I gave him a little smile.

"Hey, Katie" he popped the clip from the top of my head and dropped it into my hand. "Better."

"Thanks, Mom." My dark hair fell heavily down my back and was swept up by the warm air pushing its way from the bar.

The air swirled around me, sizzling with sensuality, caressed my arms, and tickled the small of my back. Every cell in my body synchronized their vibrations with the one moving around me. I felt alive...really alive, as though the meaning of my life lay here. In a....bar. The overwhelming sensation left no room for disappointment.

I looked up, my eyes locked with a stranger across the room. I couldn't look away, and he held my stare. Eternity passed within a few moments.

I felt disoriented and flushed and quickly turned to the bar to hide my reaction and recover.

Ken popped the top off my favorite beer and

pushed it across the counter. "Hey," he threw a curious look over my shoulder, "what the fuck was that all about?"

I gave him my 'I dunno' shrug, avoiding eye contact, and raised the bottle. "Thanks". I took a long swallow and was grateful for the sobering chill it brought to my throat and chest.

I was picking at the beer label, attempting to gather my composure, when Aiden slipped his arm around my waist. He was a doctor on my floor and had a 'thing' for me but never let it get in the way of our friendship.

"Bitch," he gave me an overly lingering hug.

"Whore," I kissed his cheek and loosened his grasp.

"Flying solo tonight?... Come on, my cousin wants to meet you." He spun me around on the bar stool.

Our eyes met again. He smiled. He was Aiden's cousin. My freshly gathered composure scattered beyond my reach. It wouldn't have mattered that Aiden was aiming me towards him, steering me with a possessive arm. I had to be near him, needed to be near him. We extended hands towards each other as Aiden introduced us. It seemed a ridiculously formal gesture, perhaps just an excuse for physical contact.

The moment our hands touched, I had a hundred flashes of him kissing me, touching me, licking me... Every cell in my body was singing like Vitas' il dolce suomo. I was losing my balance. I blinked hard. My hand was still in his; my face was on fire, my hair was sticking to the back of my neck. What the fuck, indeed.

"I'm sorry... I must be coming down with something," a weak and breathless attempt at explaining my behavior.

His brow crinkled over intensely green eyes, "You look feverish." He smiled and bent to speak against my ear as he turned me towards the door, "breathe." His voice was deep and mellow and sounded like home, like London. He held my arm as though I were about to collapse. Vitas was reaching his crescendo, I was shattering into a million shards of crystal.

The girls that had encircled him glared as he abandoned their group. If looks could kill, I would have suffered a long and painful death.

"Why'd you have to bring her over here Aiden?"... "I'm a masochist". Their voices blended with the music as we stepped outside.

His hand rested lightly on my lower back as we walked into the parking lot. I was quite a bit shorter than he, and he altered his stride to walk with me.

His touch was distracting me, clouding my mind. What was I doing with this stranger? I stopped abruptly. "I'm sorry, I didn't catch your name."

He had the most delicious, disarming smile. "Ian. Feeling better?"

I nodded, "I don't know what..."

"You just needed a bit of fresh air. Thank you for rescuing me from that lot", he looked back towards the bar "...they're all yours Aid."

"Aiden is in his element."

"Hmmm, I'd rather thought he was after you."

"Me?.. Um... I don't know... we're just friends."

Was I trying to reassure him? Why? "...and the bartender? He seemed to be a little more than chummy."

"Ken? My 'therapist'?"

"Do you always peel the labels off of your therapy?"

I nodded and laughed.

"So, why did you come out here with me?" his eyes twinkled in the moonlight.

"I... you kind of pushed me," I accused.

A smile tickled the corner of Ian's mouth, "You didn't want to get out of there?"

"I didn't say that".

Ian smiled down at me and nodded. "I felt it too."

I had to look away from his gorgeous face, his piercing gaze. "Felt what too?" My mind flickered back to the flashes of our bodies locked together. I squirmed a little.

"That bizarre attraction."

"Bizarre?... Attraction?" What?

"No, not bizarre...unexpected. Honestly, when was the last time this happened to you?"

"Never... I've never...."

"That's what I mean...me too." Ian sounded genuinely surprised.

"Well...it doesn't necessarily mean anything. ... Raging hormones? ... Or we had a few too many, or..."

"No...you only had one... and my hormones are always raging."

"You are definitely Aiden's cousin."

"Hmmph. Whatever it means...we should explore it." He spoke as if it were already decided.

"Explore our bizarre attraction to one another." I liked the idea but my head was swirling and more than capable of poor judgment. My voice of reason had been muted. "Over coffee...or perhaps a cup of tea?"

That smile again. He looked like the 'after' in a cosmetic dentistry ad, "where's your car?"

I led the way to my Jeep, and Ian held the door open as I slid in. When he shut his door, the intimacy of being enclosed was overwhelming. His rich earthy scent, and the sound of his breathing, I gripped the steering wheel to quiet my trembling hands.

Ian took a slow, deep breath as though he were scrutinizing the air. He smiled and caught my stare. "Coffee. American tea is horrid".

"Coffee." I stretched my fingers and found that I had calmed enough to drive.

Ian was squinting at my CDs, tilting them to capture the passing street lights. I wanted to reach over and touch his face but flicked the interior light on instead.

"Thank you." He slid his choice into the slot and turned off the light. I was acutely aware of his hand resting near my neck. I felt as though the tiny hairs near his hand were straining towards his touch.

The disc began to play. It was Emilie Simon's 'Desert' remix, the track I listen to when I'm all alone and feeling horny. And like Pavlov's dogs...

Jesus, why did I bring that particular disc out tonight? My body started screaming for attention; my pulse was thrumming between my legs. I shifted in my seat and tried to focus on the road ahead. Ian was watching me.

I swerved into Carms Coffee House a little too sharply causing Ian to brace himself. "Here we are," my voice was husky, I tried to clear my throat. "Coffee." I moved to jump out.

Ian held my arm before I could bolt, the heat in his touch made me shudder. I couldn't meet his stare.

He touched my forehead, "I think we should get you home... or to a Doctor."

I pushed his hand away. "Come on. Carms has the best Coffee," I didn't even drink coffee.

"No. You need some Paracetamol... and to lie down. ...perhaps I should drive?"

"I'm fine, and I'm quite able to drive!"

"Right...off we go then. Let's get you home." He was laughing at me.

"No... I'm not sure that's such a good idea. I don't know anything about you ...you might be a... a mass murderer or... "

"I'm not a mass murderer... I'm Aiden's cousin," he reasoned, innocent by association?

"That isn't particularly reassuring."

I did my best to ignore his innocent puppy look and tried to tap into my sixth sense. Was there such a thing? I felt good about this guy. "I have a shotgun under my bed."

He laughed, "Of course you do."

Ugh, Libby was home. My roommate was a pretty blond, bound with energy, loved talking, and was an infamous flirt.

Could I conjure up a look that would scare her back into her room? I didn't own any of those looks, and they wouldn't have worked if I did.

I unlocked the front door, and we stepped inside. Libby shot over like a heat-seeking missile in scrubs.

"Libby, Ian. Ian, Libby." I said flatly.

Libby dimpled and fluttered and wiggled "Damn it!...I knew I should have come out with you!"

"I didn't invite you out with me. Besides, you said you had to work tonight".

"Perhaps I should call in sick." she poked an acrylic nail at Ian's chest.

"No... you shouldn't. Aren't you already late?"

"Yeah, I'm just leaving. See you in the morning". Libby grabbed her keys and coffee "Be good!" she winked at Ian and dashed out the door.

She never failed to shock me. Ian didn't appear to take any notice of her antics.

We were alone. I fought the urge to move into Ian's arms and felt embarrassed by the surge of physical need. "Um....Coffee?... or would you like something else?... to drink," I added quickly. I clinked through some bottles "Tequila, Gin, a few different reds...or there's some Blue Moon in the fridge."

"Blue Moon? I'll try that. Thanks." He still had a curious look on his face. "Where's your stereo?" he asked, holding up that disc. I hadn't noticed him whisk it out of the car.

No, no, no. "I have tons of other CDs...look," I maneuvered him towards the living room and stereo.

"I want... " he easily held the disc out of my reach as I grabbed it "...I want to see that look again. Your emotions...feelings are written all over your face."

Oh God. "How entertaining for you," I mumbled to the floor.

Ian tipped my face up with a finger to my chin "It's beautiful".

I shook my head and escaped for the beers. For a special touch and to stall I poured the beer into tall glasses from the freezer and added a slice of orange.

When I returned, Ian sat in the middle of the couch, arms spread across the back, legs apart, and bent at the knee. A guy pose and he looked fucking gorgeous. His head was back, and his eyes were closed. Nicely dressed, casual chic - buttoned shirt, perfectly fitting jeans... He'd placed his classy lace ups neatly under the coffee table. At some point during my studies, he'd opened his eyes and was smiling at me.

"Here you go." I handed him the frosty glass and moved to the end of my suddenly small couch.

"Thank you." he took a massive gulp and grimaced, "it's very...cold." He licked a little foam from his upper lip and rubbed his chest.

I smiled, "I could nuke it ... make you feel more at home."

"No, it's perfect... I'm really not very fond of warm beer", he chuckled

I sat sideways on the couch, drawing my knees up under my chin. Another disc was playing softly in the background. "So, tell me about yourself."

He did. He spoke of his parents and home outside of London, his younger brothers and sisters - I got the impression that he had a large family.

He continued on, "My Father is arranging for me to take over the...the family business. I never felt ready or...powerful enough. I don't know, maybe everything has changed...now."

"And you?" He stifled my question. "Tell me everything."

I shared memories of growing up in California and moving to England. Time spent in London studying Nursing, my family's home in Gloucestershire.

"Gloucestershire. That's a beautiful county -- the commons are quite vast...peaceful. There's a quaint castle overlooking the Wye. My brothers and I used to play there until it was converted into a prison." Ian smiled at the memories.

"St Briavel's Castle overlooks the River Wye, it's quite near my Parents' home. I think it was a prison up until eighteen-something. It's a youth hostel now.

"Hmmm, we're not speaking of the same place...obviously. Tell me, why did you move back to the States...to this town."

"I was ...restless. I felt as though I'd been searching for something. I chose this town by sticking a pin in a map -- literally."

Ian nodded, "fate."

We spoke for hours through several glasses of beer and countless shuffled songs. We grew increasingly at ease and familiar.

Our conversation reached a lull, a silent moment as a disc whirled to the next random tract.

That song. I could immediately feel the heat rising through my body. I felt his eyes on me, watching me struggle. The music no longer held the same association. Now it was about him, and it was a hundred times worse.

Ian touched my face, urging me to look at him. I expected to see his smile, but his face had changed, taking on a hungry, wild look. Not unlike my own, I imagine.

Ian leaned over me and touched his lips to mine, an unspoken question. I answered, opening to his tongue's exploration, my own following eagerly. My fingers traced the contours of his face, caught on the sharp, unshaven slope of his jaw, and delighted at the silky coolness of his chocolate locks. Ian twisted his fingers taut in my hair, pulling a moan from my throat as his tongue plunged deeper.

Ian leaned back and maneuvered my hips to straddle his. I folded my legs on either side of him and planted myself on his imprisoned cock. I shifted, and he groaned, pulling me down firmly, and anchoring me. Feeling him beneath me, so close to where I needed him to be, caused any remaining shreds of restraint and modesty to flee, and something raw and basic emerged.

"Ian." I barely recognized my voice; it sounded desperate. I tugged at his shirt, and he flew through his buttons. I pushed it from his shoulders and leaned into him. I kissed the hollow of his neck and tasted him with a swirl of my tongue. I continued along his collar bone and over the muscled ridge of his shoulder, savoring his skin's slightly salty flavor and fiery heat.

Ian shook his arms free of his shirt and held my head in his hands. He crushed my mouth against his and roughly plunged his tongue between my lips. I dug my fingers into his back, needing to get closer and moaned into his mouth. His hands flew to my hips as I pushed myself onto him. He slid his hands down the back of my jeans and dragged me forward.

Ian's cock bucked beneath me, causing ice crystals to race up my spine and across my skin. My heart was pounding in my ears and against his hardness.

Ian pulled my shirt over my head and threw it to the floor. He followed the flow of my hair and pushed it from my breasts, kissing along the curves, lifting them to his mouth. His thumbs grazed my nipples, drawing a moan from my throat. He nibbled and tugged through the lace, sending lightning bolts through my core. I buried my face in his hair; he smelled like exotic herbs and mysterious forests. I wanted everything he could give me. I needed him to take everything I had.

I pulled away from him and looked into his dark eyes as I slid down from his lap. I unzipped his jeans as he pulled everything down and kicked his legs free. His cock sprang loose and slapped my cheek, leaving a little splatter.

"Sorry," he wiped it away with his finger. I pulled his hand back to me and slowly licked his fingers. One tasted dark and spicy - I sucked it into my mouth. I wanted more.

His legs were on either side of me as I kneeled before him. He leaned back into the cushions and watched me. I sat back on my heels as I ran my fingers along his muscled calves and kissed the insides of his knees. I licked and kissed his thighs; his muscles flexed beneath my tongue. His response and my hunger drove me.

I reached his balls and ran the tip of my tongue

lightly along their underside and continued up his shaft. Ian's long fingers dug into the soft cushions, and a rumble rose from his chest. Some small part of me had been screaming warnings and was horrified by my behavior. But completely ignored, it grew silent.

I cupped his balls, feeling their weight, and steadied his cock in my other hand. Its velvet head was glistening. I ran the tip of my tongue along the slit; the taste was intoxicating. Ian growled as I popped his head into my mouth and swirled my tongue around its rim. I slowly slid down until I couldn't breathe and swallowed. He pulsated against my lips and grew even larger. I held his shaft in both hands as I rose and followed my mouth to the top, my tongue exploring every detail. He was slick with saliva and as hard as granite. I moaned over his head as my tongue gathered another spicy sample. Ian's hands twisted in my hair as I licked.

"Stand..." His voice was deeper and strained. "...Stand up."

I reluctantly left my post and stood before him, panting with desire.

He held my hips, a bruising grip, and pushed his forehead into my belly. I ran my fingers through his hair and sensed his struggle.

Ian looked up into my confused eyes, "if we go any further, I won't be able to control myself... I won't be able to stop. You're not...ready for me".

I rocked my hips in his hands, "I feel pretty...ready."

Ian breathed deep and growled, "That's not what I mean".

"You don't want to...? You don't want me?" I was trying hard not to sound crushed.

"What?...No! Christ!" Ian pulled me to him; his breath was searing my neck. "It's taking everything I've got not to rip the rest of your clothes off with my teeth and bury myself in you, deep and hard, claim you as mine alone." Ian's teeth grazed my neck sharply, "I want you to scream my name as you come. I want you to give yourself to me...completely. And you're not ready."

I was about to argue when tires crunched along the drive. "Bugger! It's Libby." I scooped up his clothes and pushed him into my room. I threw my PJ t-shirt on and went to warn Libby that Ian was still here.

"So you don't want me to strut around in my bra and thong?" Libby strutted in demonstration.

"No.... not really...ever."

Libby laughed and then noticed that I was still in my jeans. "That's not good"

"Yeah, well. ... I'm going to bed. Good night Lib."

Libby pouted and gave me a hug, patting my head. "It's okay honey; maybe you'll get lucky tonight."

I heard a chuckle from my room.

I brushed my teeth and washed up a little. I was exhausted. I slipped into my sweat pants and found Ian sound asleep half-covered with my duvet. He'd put his boxers on.

I slipped in beside him and was immediately enveloped by his heat. He rolled onto his side and slipped his arm across my tummy. "G'night Kate," he mumbled.

That was the first time he spoke my name.

I woke to the sounds of Libby's giggles and Ian's deep laughter. "Nice... she's already working her magic." I grabbed some clothes and snuck into the bathroom. I showered and threw on a little makeup, Vicky Secrets, Jeans and a light sweater. I guess I looked okay. I padded out to the kitchen, worried that I might be greeted with indifference. "g'morning".

Ian smiled and his eyes sparkled and crinkled. "Good morning." he pulled me to him and kissed me. He was wearing his jeans and his unbuttoned shirt exposed his magnificent chest and abs. I fastened two of his shirt buttons, and he chuckled.

Libby watched us over the rim of her lipstick blotched coffee cup. "Ian was telling me that he was a model in London."

"Really? You didn't tell me that."

"No... I did one photo shoot. Black and white artsy work. I think the guy was bent...some of the poses were... well..."

"I made him pose for me!" God, Libby is at her finest. Ian buttoned a few more buttons.

"Coffee?" Ian offered.

"She doesn't drink coffee." Libby said as though confirming my oddness.

Ian sat me down and handed me a glass of OJ; his fingers lingered over mine.

"Thank you. Where are you off to looking all glam Lib?" I was thinking it was for Ian's benefit.

"My sister's, in Boston... just for the weekend"

Ian was resting his hand on my thigh - he gave it a squeeze with that news. I ignored it.

"Do you need a ride to the airport?"

"Thanks, no. Aiden's going to take me."

"I asked him to bring my things over too." Ian gave me an apologetic look.

"Your things"

Ian grimaced.

"All of your things?"

Ian nodded.

"Geeze, I bet he's pissed. Aren't you supposed to be visiting him?"

"You can't make Ian spend an entire two weeks with Aiden. That would be a total waste. I told him he could stay with us. Aren't you off for the next couple of weeks anyway? It's perfect!" Libby smiled sweetly at Ian and got up "I've got to finish packing," she ruffled Ian's hair as she passed.

"Moving in?" I was angry with myself for sounding hopeful.

"Are you angry?" Ian gathered me to him and kissed my neck before I could answer. "Mmmm, you smell like rain ...and lilacs... and Kate. I could eat you for breakfast".

"I'm not angry, and I'm not on the menu".

Ian raised an eyebrow in an 'oh really' expression, "Do you mind if I shower first? I'm a little ripe."

He wasn't. He was making my mouth water, "The towels are in that cupboard."

Ian sang while he showered, tweaking some of my out-of-tune heart strings.

The door bell rang. Aiden had a large leather suitcase in tow and a leather back pack slung over his shoulder.

"Bitch" he pecked me on the lips.

"Whore." I guess we were still friends.

Aiden gave me an accusing glare.

"What?"

He raised his brows. "Fine fucking mess you've gotten yourself into."

"Um... I seem to remember you orchestrating this... and it isn't a mess. "

"Oh?" He seemed surprised.

Ian entered the room wearing a floral towel around his waist, freshly showered and god-like.

"What the fuck?" Aiden indicated the towel.

"Yeah, I know....flowers. You've got my clothes." They did the guy hug thing. "Aid... thanks, Man."

"Yeah. Good to see you, for what...an hour?"

"There's no way you'd see any action with me around." Ian teased.

"Fuck off Gooseberry." They laughed.

Ian grabbed his bags. "Call me...we'll do something," he instructed Aiden circling his finger in the air to include the three of us and left to dress.

"He's a cocky fucker" Aiden looked at me "...you're attracted to that?"

"Yeah Aiden... that's what I look for in a guy."

"Bitch."

"Whore."

Libby pushed through the bedroom door with her abundant matching red luggage.

"Holy fuck Lib! I thought you were just going for the weekend!"

"Shut up, Aiden, and help me... we're going to be late." "You're going to be late, my timing is perfect."

They left with doors slamming and abuse flying.

Alone again.

My tummy rumbled, nervous and hungry. I went to the kitchen and sliced some fruit into two bowls added a dollop of organic yogurt and a perfect strawberry for each top.

I dug in at the table while blindly flicking through one of Libby's magazines. Fine fucking mess I've gotten myself into - Aiden's words echoed in my head.

I knew, without a doubt, that I didn't have the power to resist Ian. If he wanted to hang around for a couple of weeks, then that's how it would be. I'd just have to deal with the aftermath...after. Resignation calmed my stomach and nerves somewhat.

I stuffed a large chunk of apple in my mouth just as Ian walked in. Hair stylishly tousled, loose jeans hanging on his hips, a hint of boxers, a bare chest, and a shirt flapping behind him. I started choking and spluttering. Ian smacked my back and grabbed a glass of water.

"Jesus... you know what you look like! Are you trying to kill me??!" I took a tentative sip.

"What do I look like?" he sucked his cheeks in and angled his shoulders, completing the cat walk look.

We laughed. "If that's what you gave Libby, I'm surprised she didn't jump you."

"Your friend is a nutter."

"Yes, she is," I agreed. "Are you hungry?" I handed him his bowl of fruit.

"I don't know," he poked the fruit with a finger "... I'm not really a fruit kind of guy...but you make it

look so delicious with the choking and gagging... "
he smiled and started munching.

I sat with him while he ate. His jaw was fascinating to watch, chewing - it looked like it could crush bones.

He scooped up his last mandarin segment and stretched over to me. "Open. I want to feed you."

I obeyed. My center was catching on fire.

"Come here." Ian pulled me to him as I awkwardly swallowed. He kissed my lips lightly, then retreated slightly. He wanted me to come to him. I leaned into him and kissed his closed lips, my tongue begging entry. I felt him smile before he opened it to me. He resumed command, sliding his hands up from my hips to my waist, lifting my sweater above my tummy. He licked and nibbled my exposed flesh, giving rise to a mass of goose bumps and shivers. He unzipped my jeans without interruption and let them pool around my feet.

He bit my panties and yanked; they snapped and fell to the floor in tatters. I want to tear your clothes off with my teeth... his earlier words echoed. I quickly pulled my expensive sweater up and off. Once it cleared my face, I found myself staring at my gawking neighbor through my French doors. I gasped, and Ian turned and growled. Mr. Williams quickly left his pruning and retreated into his home.

I looked into Ian's eyes and promptly forgot about Mr. What's-his-name, who continued to peek through his curtains.

Ian cupped my neatly shaved mound and stroked my pussy. I knew I was as wet as April rains.

"Ready enough for you now?" I asked timidly.

Ian smiled as his fingers dipped and twirled. "That's not what I meant." His expression grew serious, "I'm sorry about last night. I...I just couldn't."

I wanted to ask why but didn't want to spoil the moment.

"The moon."

"Sorry?"

"You want to know why...it was because of the full moon."

Ian's expression remained serious, contradicting his silly words, leaving me confused.

"Here," Ian slipped out of his shirt and held it for me to slip into. "Your neighbor is still watching us."

I peeked over Ian's shoulder and caught the twitch of a curtain. "Perve", I mumbled.

"I don't know...you're the one exposing your naked... dripping... delicious... body to anyone who should pass by." Ian was kissing my shoulders between his words.

I blushed at the realization of my behavior. He was making me act like a starving sex fiend.

Ian grinned, "sex fiend?"

My blush grew deeper, "did I say that out loud? I...."

"No. " Ian studied my face and looked torn. "Come here." He led me to my dark living room -- the curtains were still drawn. "Sit." He looked at me for a long while before speaking.

"The attraction we feel for each other...It may seem a simple peculiarity to you ...but it's far more...complicated...than that. We have a special...bond, you and I." He was treading lightly and making me nervous.

I frowned.

"Kate", Listen to me... Listen to me.

I was listening to him, and his lips weren't moving.

Please try not to be upset. I'll explain everything...somehow.

"Don't be upset?! What...how are you doing that? I'm losing my fucking mind!!"

No, you're not losing your mind. It's our connection. "Connection? What do you mean? I don't understand!" Kate.

"Stop it! It's freaking me out. Tell me what's going on. Explain this to me...please."

"I never thought I'd have to explain this to a human, I..."

"A human! What do you think you are?!"

"Please, Kate! I don't know how to do this."

"Just fucking tell me."

"I'm a werewolf."

"What? A what?? Jesus fucking Christ. You need to leave."

Look at me, Kate.

Ian discarded his jeans. Kate moved towards the phone but was halted by a vicious growl.

Wait. Ian bent over and let out a piercing yelp as his bones crackled and muscles contorted, he shook as his skin transformed into a dark chocolate glistening pelt.

A huge wolf stood before me, panting, tongue lolling from the side of his mouth. Familiar green eyes were looking into mine.

"Holy shit...fuck. No...no...no. Ian? No...this can't

fucking be happening."

It padded over to me, claws clicking on the hardwood floor. I backed up into a corner and sank to the floor. It nudged my hand with its nose.

Kate, it's me.

I cautiously placed my hand on the wolf's head, "Ian?"

Yes. Ian licked my palm, his tongue long and rough.

"Please...change back...I think I'm going to lose it." I closed my eyes, releasing hot tears, and started to shake uncontrollably.

Ian returned to his human form as quickly and slipped back into his clothes.

He kissed my tears and held me tight. "It's okay...its okay. Shhhh... Let me tell you our story, how we came to be, what we are today."

I nodded but kept my eyes tightly shut. Ian began his story as it was told to him as a child. He continued and described how at one time weres protected crops in Europe and the native Americans' beloved Caribou. He spoke of witch trials in Estonia in the 1600s that resulted in the destruction of nearly 100 weres.

"We quickly sank into myth and legend for our own preservation. There are many writings featuring werewolves and films, most of which are rubbish."

Questions flooded my mind. "Do you eat....people?"

"No! No. I do crave meat, but I get it from a shop just like you. And I'm not very fond of fruit."

"So, you're not going to eat me...what are you doing with me?"

Ian laughed, "I might have if your neighbor hadn't interrupted."

"Wha....Oh. Hmmph"

"We all have our other halves wandering around out there, particularly true for weres. " Ian searched Kate's face for sign of encouragement, but the confused look persisted. "Your scent, your flavor...they make my heart scream for you, make me feel alive. You are my other half...my mate."

"I am your...mate?"

"Yes."

"What if I don't want to be?"

"Then I'll leave, broken hearted with my tail between my legs. But the feeling is mutual. I knew it the moment I first saw you. You felt it too." Ian waited patiently while Kate did her best to understand.

"Would you have ...changed... last night if we hadn't stopped?"

"Yes, I believe I would have. It was a full moon; my wolf was near the surface and wanted to take you."

"What do you mean?"

"Make the bond permanent. I wouldn't have been able to leave after that. I want to give you the choice."

"You can't control your...wolf during a full moon?"

"Normally, I can, but not around you."

"If I choose...if you make the um, bond permanent... how do we live? As outcasts?"

"No. I spend most of my time in my human form. We would appear as... husband and wife." Ian half expected to see Kate cringe, but she didn't.

"What about...babies?"

Ian caught the image of a litter of puppies from Kate's mind.

"No. No puppies...perhaps twins, and we can't change until after puberty. "

"Our children would be werewolves?" I couldn't believe I was asking these questions. I wanted to laugh hysterically but couldn't.

"Yes, but more human and more powerful than I." "Will I change into a ...a werewolf?"

"No."

"If you bit me?"

"No! " Ian answered abruptly, putting an end to that line of questioning.

"Is Aiden like you?"

The question annoyed Ian, "No, he's nothing like me. Yes, he is a were."

"Does he know about us...that you think I'm your... mate?"

"I know that you are, and yes he does. He could tell in the bar...that's why he had his hands all over you...to piss me off."

"Oh."

"How old are you?" I asked, vaguely recalling some werewolf stories.

"You don't want to know."

"Now I definitely want to know. 40?"

Ian frowned, "Do I look 40?!"

"No." I studied his face. "Late 20s, early 30s, I suppose. You're not like vampires, are you? Hundreds of years old?" I smiled.

"Yes."

"I was joking. Wait.... are vampires are real,

too??" "Yes."

My world was changing into one of monsters and nightmares. Would I miss 'normal', 'mundane', and 'boring'? Is this what I'd been searching for? It seemed to be. Life with a wolf, an old...

"How... old...are you?"

"I was born in 1615. "

"Sixteen...fifteen. More than three hundred years older than me. I'm having a hard time wrapping my head around all of this."

"I know."

"So, when I'm, say...8o, you'll still look like this?"

"More or less."

"Well. That's not going to work, is it!"

"I'll still love you when you're old and wrinkly."

"You love me?"

"Yes."

"How can you possibly know that after what...not even 24 hours."

"You feel the same way."

"What I feel is confused."

"About all of this....but not about me."

"Aiden is right! You are a cocky fucker!"

"You and I are made for each other and weres know, absolutely know, when they meet their mate. It's as simple as that."

"But I'm not like you....I'm not a werewolf. "

"No, but you feel it too."

"Hmmff. But there's no way that we can stay together. I'm going to be too old for you."

"I'll always be 300 years older than you."

"But you don't look old."

"You know, I learned all of this over years and

years. You're trying to compress it into hours. I want you to forget about all of these details and just answer one question for me."

"What?"

"Do you want to be with me? If for some reason you don't I'll have to get out of here while I still can."

"Jesus. Yes. Yes, I do, today. I don't know about tomorrow or the rest of my life!"

"You're being too cerebral. Okay. Today. We'll figure tomorrow out when it gets here."

I smiled. Tiny steps maybe I could deal with tiny steps.

"I'm starving. Come on, no more fruit. Give me something bloody and rare!"

"Eww."

"I'm joking a little. A steak would be lovely."

Chapter 2

IAN and KATE and LIBBY

I think there may be some steak in the freezer", I rummaged through the frozen bricks and pulled out a couple of suspects. "Libby's, I'm sure she wouldn't mind. I think she fancies you."

"Hmphh."

"You don't find her ... attractive?" Was I feeling jealous?

"Kate," he laughed at me, " I can't be attracted to another...woman, not now."

I detected his hesitation, "another ... um ... wolf ... ess?"

"Wolfess?" he chuckled. "No. Its you. You've put an end to my sweet, sweet bachelor days," Ian feigned remorse.

"I'm sure that you've seen far more than your fair share of those. Three hundred years and change? It really is about time you settled down. You should probably be checked out by your Vet too." I lectured.

"My Rabies shots are up to date...and I'm as clean as a whistle in all other areas as well." Ian declared, giving me a wink.

"Hmmph."

"You know," Ian became pensive, "I'd more or less given up on the idea of finding....you. Some time ago, I began to think that my mate was an agoraphobic hiding in a remote little nowhere village in an obscure corner of the Earth. I wasn't going to meet her...ever. Then last night ..." Ian smiled, "I sensed you immediately, even before you entered the bar... I wanted to howl with pure joy ... then I realized you were ... human."

"You were disappointed."

"Disappointed?" Ian frowned. "How could I be? I've been waiting for you, hunting for you - at times... for centuries. I was surprised that your scent wasn't Were, that my other half would be so soft and weak, so human."

"I am not soft and weak." I gave him a mighty yet completely ineffective shove, proving his point rather than making my own.

Ian laughed, "exactly."

I sighed softly and weakly. "We're ill matched on so many different levels. You're so big and old...and a wolf for God's sake. Can't you just ask for a retrial on this whole mate thing?"

"No. I can't. It is what it is. It doesn't matter at all that you're a tiny, cynophobic, fruit loving, sex crazed human child. We're stuck with each other and..."

"Sex crazed?"

"...and I have never been happier. Yes...sex crazed. I'm very happy about that part."

Ian smiled. The direction of his gaze made me realize that I'd been walking around knickerless, barely clothed in his unbuttoned shirt. I spotted my shredded wodge of lace under the table. Heat raced to my cheeks with the memory, and the insides of my thighs were beginning to feel slick. I pulled Ian's shirt tighter around my body.

"I'm sorry I ruined your lingerie." Ian seemed to be acutely aware of my excited state, his eyes darkened and closed, he lifted his nose, his nostrils flaring. God, he could probably smell my arousal. He cleared his throat and turned away from me. Ian grabbed the steaks and tapped them on the edge of the counter, "I don't think I can wait for these to thaw...shall we eat out?" Ian avoided eye contact and moved towards the hallway.

My wild inner creature had escaped and refused to be re-caged. I hopped ahead of him and into the doorway, blocking his passage. I raised my arms and rested them on either side of the door frame, causing Ian's shirt to open and expose my nearly bare body.

"How long are you planning on keeping me waiting?"

Before I could finish asking, Ian was crushing me against his bare chest, demanding access to my hungry mouth, bruising my lips. He straightened his back, and my toes lost contact with the floor. I wrapped my legs around him as he moved us to my room, and he awkwardly removed the rest of my clothes. Crashing into the door frame, I slammed against his body, and we both moaned. Ian threw me on my bed and followed, looming over me on hands and knees.

Ian panted, "I thought you'd be too upset by...everything I didn't think you'd want...."

"I want you... " I unzipped his jeans and slid my hand along the bulge in his boxers, "please."

Ian removed his jeans and boxers, tossing them

into a corner. He stood completely naked before me, beautiful, like an angel. I sat up to touch him, confirm his existence, and prove that I wasn't dreaming. Ian brought my hand up to his lips, my eyes followed and met his deep emerald pools, dark with desire.

"Lay down," a gently spoken command.

As I leaned back, Ian lifted my knees and opened my legs. His eyes lingered on my mouth and then traveled down to my exposed sex. My breathing grew ragged as I watched. Ian brought his head down, placed his tongue near my pucker, and dragged it up through my glistening folds and over my hooded nub. He drank of me as a butterfly at a flower, a giant wolf butterfly. My fingers twisted in his hair as he teased and nibbled and sucked, drawing me closer to the edge.

Ian replaced his tongue with his hand, his fingers and thumb finding my most sensitive points and depths.

He kissed me urgently; his tongue continued to plunge and caress. I could taste myself on his lips. The sensations began to swirl and gather and collide. My hips were moving greedily against his fingers.

Ian moved his lips to my ear." come for me, Kate." I could do nothing else. I crashed and shattered and whimpered as he kissed me, his fingers drawing out the tremors.

I was not lulled or soothed. My body did not purr with satisfaction. The flood gates were ripped from their hinges, letting loose a torrent of sharply defined desire. "Please ..." words were elusive, I pleaded with my eyes. I moved his hand from my wetness and shuddered with the loss. "Please."

Ian raised himself over me and opened my legs further with his knees; the sudden coolness made me shiver. Ian easily restrained my arms above my head and perched himself at my entrance, his head hot and threatening. I raised my hips in a desperate attempt to capture him but could not. Ian looked into my eyes, drew me into his thoughts. Not to hear his unspoken words but to feel his desire, to experience his overwhelming need. It hit me like a colossal iceberg, crowded my mind with his absolute hunger. My body began to shudder, and Ian seized this moment to plunge into my depths. I came in great waves, exploding from my center...ripping through me. I cried out against his neck, "Ian holy fuck."

Ian growled into my ear "mine."

"Yes." I agreed gasping. Nothing could have been more obvious at that moment.

Ian raised himself, letting my arms loose, and remained still within me for a time. My freed fingers danced over his muscled hills and valleys, and Ian began a slow ascent, leaving a feeling of emptiness behind. In an unjustified panic my fingers dug into his sides, pulling him back to me.

Ian obliged and filled me, then picked up a rhythm that my body matched, thrust for thrust.

My fingers found purchase in his hair, and he dipped down to lick my lips. My tongue met his and the connection drove him deeper. My eyes fluttered shut and an image of Ian pounding me from behind flashed through my mind. Whether it originated in his mind or my own, I couldn't tell.

Ian swiftly withdrew, rolled me over and raised my hips. He pressed my shoulders into the bed and moved my knees further apart. I was completely exposed and pointing to the heavens. I expected the pounding to begin as in my vision, but instead felt kisses on either cheek and then a rough, hot tongue lapping up my juices. It didn't feel like Ian's, it felt like his wolf.

I was seized by fear.

Kate his tongue continued the tortuous licking. I'm still here. Ian's hands ran down my back - I didn't feel claws and relaxed. I won't change again until it's needed or you ask me to.

I couldn't imagine ever asking him to change.

Ian positioned himself behind me, and I wiggled an invitation.

"Look...look in your mirror."

I lifted my head and found myself looking into my perfectly though innocently angled dresser mirror. The site of our glistening bodies made me catch my breath and set me ablaze.

Ian entered me as we watched. He sheathed himself to the hilt. The sensation, the vision...it was overwhelming, too much. I tried to rock forward, to move away, but Ian held my hips firmly in place. His movements became determinedly languid, allowing my body to accept him fully. The pseudo pain quickly transformed into utter bliss, and I began to rock and sway with him. Ian unleashed the power he had been keeping tightly reined. I buried my face in the twisted bed clothes and screamed his name as he pummeled me.

"No...not yet Kate," Ian slowed to let me recover

slightly. His hands traveled over my thighs and hips and up my back, I moaned under their heat. He looped an arm under mine and pulled me upright. His large hands covered my breasts. "You're beautiful."

I looked up into the mirror but looked away quickly. The scene was too intimate, too sexual for casual observation. It spurred my arousal even higher. I twisted and reached back, and our lips and tongues reunited. I purred, reveling in his sweetness. Ian growled as I nibbled his bottom lip.

He pressed my shoulders back down into the bed and his grinding picked up its pace. He changed his angle slightly and I would have jumped off the bed if he hadn't had me in his iron grip.

"Ian..." I whimpered. "I'm going to c....come."

Ian entwined his hand in my hair and had me rise on hands and knees. He leaned over and kissed my shoulder. "Yes...come with me Kate now." Ian bit into my shoulder as our bodies shuddered and clenched. The brief sting of his bite blended with overwhelming pleasure as Ian poured himself into me.

My body was trembling uncontrollably and my limbs turned to jelly. Ian rolled us onto our sides as we collapsed.

We lay entwined and connected in the mess of bedclothes. Stripes of late afternoon sun pierced the blinds, covering us in a distorted zebra pattern.

Ian held me tightly against his chest and kissed my still tender shoulder. "I'm sorry...I couldn't stop myself."

"Your wolf?"

"Emmm...we've marked you as ours." Ian buried his face in my hair "Thank God I found you..." his voice cracked, "I thought I never... "

"I know... " I pressed my back against his chest and kissed his fingers, "...I guess I'd been searching for you too."

LIBBY

Libby grew impatient and annoyed with incompetent airline staff, fumbling with her luggage, smacking their gum in her face. "Jesus! Where do they find you people?"

"Ma'am?"

"Never mind. Give me that...I'll push it myself." She dismissed the help with a flick of her hand.

Libby spotted her twin standing near her car in the '10 minute parking zone' having an animated conversation with the airport police.

"Damn it! Don't you have terrorists to catch...I tell you, my sister will...here she is now!" She scowled and trotted over to Libby donning a brilliant smile.

"Lib! You look absolutely gorgeous!!" She kissed her sister's cheeks.

"And so do you Anna!" Libby returned the kisses. They were identical twins.

"So, tell me what all the excitement is about." Anna stuffed Libby's luggage into the trunk of her BMW. "The suspense has been killing me. I don't know why you couldn't just tell me over the phone." They climbed into the car.

Anna sped off, tires squealing, honking at a pedestrian attempting to cross her path.

"Anna! Jesus! You're going to get us killed!! Or get yourself a nice Manslaughter charge." Libby clicked her belt in place.

"Never mind my driving; tell me what's going on." "You won't bloody believe it!"

"Libby!"

"Alright, alright,"Libby grinned from ear to ear. "I had an Alpha Male in my house...under my roof!"

"What?! How? How do you know?"

"Katie brought him home. Can you believe it?"

"Katie? Why would.... How do you know that it was a Were?"

"I've been chasing Weres all of my adult life...I know a wolf when I smell one. " Libby crinkled her nose.

"Okay, how do you know that it's an Alpha?"

"Because he's a stuck up, over confident son-of-a- bitch."

"Well, yeah, it would be a son of a bitch." Anna grinned. "Right."

"What was it after? Surely not Katie."

"I don't know, I think so... maybe."

"Did it catch on to what you are?" Anna frowned, concerned for her sister.

"No. I'm always careful not to smell my work and I never work at home. Besides, I charmed his pants off." Libby declared smugly.

Anna raised her brows. "Oh?"

"Okay, not quite... but I could have."

"I have no doubt unless it is after Kate. What are you going to do? This is exactly what you've been waiting for."

"I know. That's why I'm here... I need your help Anna." "God Lib." Anna groaned.

"I know, I know. Pleeeese Anna, I really need

your help."

"Geeze. Do you have a plan? Any ideas?"

Libby looked timidly towards her sister, "When is the next blue moon?"

"What?" Anna glanced at her sister in horror. "No Lib. You've got to be joking. It'll rip your throat out!!"

"No, I think it'll work."

I woke a little disoriented amidst the chaos of the twisted duvet. I stretched and discovered a few unusual aches in few unusual places. It was dark and seemed late at night but I could smell and hear food cooking. Mmmm steak. Ian. Memories of the previous hours flooded my mind.

I was a little shocked and horrified by this new me but more than that, I was happy. Happily hooked up with a wolf-man, yeah, that part was strange, but I could put it away in a little box and deal with it later.

The scent of perfectly seasoned steak tickled my nose again, and my tummy growled demanding attention.

"I can hear your stomach from over here!"

I smiled and rolled out of bed, grabbing a robe from my door on my way to the kitchen. Ian had set the table simply and elegantly, with a single Iris as the center piece. "That's my favorite flower." I stepped into his arms.

"Really? I think it's your neighbor's favorite as well." He gave me a wicked smile.

"What? You picked that from Mr. Williams' garden?"

"Now he'll have something else to gawk at."

"He'll think I've been stealing from his flower

bed!"

"No, he won't. You're the image of innocence. No, you're right. I'd almost forgotten your little show for him."

"Please, don't remind me. I'll never be able to look him in the eye again."

Ian got that wolfish 'I'm going to eat you' look and untied my robe. "Do you think Mr. Williams is ready for part two?"

"Stop it! We have to eat something else besides each other, or we'll die. That'll spoil all your fun."

Ian smiled and pulled my seat from beneath the table, "Mademoiselle."

I sat and was served a perfect filet with a perfect salad. Ian's plate had three filets and a healthy serving of lettuce. "I thought you didn't like to eat anything green or colorful."

"I don't, but I want to be a regular sort of guy," he winked and stuffed a Heimlich worthy chunk of meat in his mouth.

"There's nothing regular about you Ian." I sliced into the steak -- medium rare, just how I like it. "Do you do dishes and laundry too?"

"No, I don't. I have people who do that sort of thing. I enjoy cooking."

Wealthy huh? "Are you a spoiled brat?"

"No, but I always get what I want," he pointed at me with his fork "eventually." Ian stopped eating for a moment. "You could have all the money in the world and not be happy. Love is the only thing that truly matters."

"Those are rare words to come out of a man's mouth."

"Yeah, you learn all sorts of difficult lessons given unlimited time."

We finished eating in comfortable silence and watched the sun rise. Ian cleared the table, leaving only the solitary Iris in the crystal vase. He herded me out of the kitchen. "How about a relaxing bath and then a trip into town? We have some shopping to do."

Aiden was riding his Harley out of town, speeding to nowhere in particular. He'd been partying with his Vamp friends, indulging in their specialty -- Bloody Marys. Nothing virgin about their version of the classic. Vamp blood always gave him a mad case of insomnia, perfect when he was on call but a nuisance otherwise.

He rode helmetless and always too fast. He likened it to letting his wolf free but without the effort. Not that he was lazy. He was a damn good doctor, worked his ass off. He just didn't put a lot of energy into other areas. Work, ass, and getting shit-faced -- his priorities, not necessarily in that order.

His family did not tolerate his habits and associations, he had in effect, been disowned by all except Ian. They had remained loyal to each other throughout.

Aiden was pleased that Ian had finally found his mate and that he had been the one to introduce them. He was also delighted that it was Kate, though he would like to have gotten a taste. No chance now, not that a chance existed before. Maybe now that he wouldn't be sniffing around Kate, he could stay away from Libby. She was an annoying bitch, but he kept coming back for more and he could not fathom why.

As he surfaced from his thoughts, he recognized a house as he sped by. He braked and let the back of his bike slide, cutting a half-moon in the gravel. He revved the oversized engine, a deep throaty sound he loved, and returned to the familiar house. He studied the steps, the porch and the door as he sat on his idling bike. He remembered in a flash of images -- Claire. A sexy redhead who was always game for a little fun, but booted him out when she thought things were getting a little too serious.

One of the lights was on, that was invitation enough. Aiden silenced his beast and dismounted, its engine 'tinked' as it cooled and was soon joined by a volley of lofty Cicadas . Aiden bound up the porch steps and gave the door a few taps with his knuckles. The door opened, and a young woman appeared. Aiden blinked; she had the same red hair though it was cut short. She had the same curves though leaner, and the same eyes, but it wasn't Claire.

The girl gave Aiden the same 'once over' and planted her hand on her hip, "Can I help you?" she asked in an unhelpful tone.

"I um, I was looking for Claire."

"Claire?" The girl's voice softened, "Claire was my Grandmother; this was her house. " Her eyes clouded, "she passed away a few years ago. I live here now." She looked up and frowned. "Who are you? How did you know my Gran?"

This wasn't the first instance Aiden had been tricked by time, but it was disconcerting none the less. "I...we, she used to watch me, when I was a child. I used to sleep over sometimes, in the blue room. Nearly everything was cornflower blue." Aiden tried to recall little details to help support his story, but glorious fucking was really all that came to mind. He shut up.

The girl continued to frown.

"I'm sorry, my name is Aiden."

She shook his hand briefly. "I'm Zoe." She looked up at Aiden curiously, "my Grandfather's name was Aiden. That's odd isn't it? Aiden isn't a very common name." She studied his face. "Would you like to come in?"

"You shouldn't invite strangers into your house you know."

"I can take care of myself," Zoe claimed in a grim, not boastful tone.

Aiden sat on Claire's sofa, now faded and tatty. Zoe was digging through a desk drawer, shuffling through a mass of papers. "A-ha!" She held a photograph up, and her expression grew serious. She handed it to Aiden. "You look like him."

"Who is this?" Aiden didn't really want to know; he wanted to leave. He rose from the sofa.

"He was my father, Alexander."

"Holy Fuck." Aiden Alexander fell back into the cushions.

"He was your father too, wasn't he. That makes sense with Gran babysitting you and your name and everything." Zoe was putting two and two together and getting an 'F' for a fucked up situation.

No, he wasn't my father. I am his. Aiden nodded absent-mindedly.

"That makes us Brother and Sister!" Zoe plopped down next to Aiden and held his hand. "This is totally awesome! I thought I'd lost everyone."

Aiden pulled himself out of his frantic thoughts and considerations. "What happened to your...our Father?"

Zoe studied her hands. "Mom shot him in the head. Then she shot herself. I was just a kid, I don't really remember much."

"He died? What kind of bullet was it?"

"What?! I don't know. What kind a question is that?!" Zoe jumped up from the sofa.

"I'm sorry Zoe. I'm a Doctor, it's just my morbid curiosity I guess. Please forgive me."

"A Doctor? You look a little too young to be a Doctor." Zoe didn't seem at all surprised.

"Yeah, just call me Doogie."

"I don't think I will. He was a dork. You do look very young." Zoe was probing.

"What?" Aiden fidgeted and was becoming annoyed. "Thank you?"

"I look young, too." Zoe persisted, but Aiden refused to bite. "How old do I look?"

"Fuck, I don't know. Nineteen?'" Aiden didn't look up.

"No, Damn it! I'm forty-seven!" Zoe slammed her fist on the coffee table.

"So, you should be fucking thrilled to bits!" Ian stood and began to pace like a caged animal.

"No! I'm a God Damned freak! We're both freaks, aren't we?!" Zoe flopped into a chair and gathered herself into a ball. "That isn't all. I'm too strong and too fast, I can hear everything I can smell everything." Zoe began to sob, "what's wrong with me??!" She looked at Aiden through glassy eyes. "Do you know? Is it some sort of genetic mutation or...or cancer, a brain tumor?"

Aiden pulled at bunches of his hair. "No. God Damn it, no. Fuck, fuck, fuck!" Aiden kneeled at Zoe's feet and held her hands away from her face. "Look at me. No, you don't have cancer or a fucking brain tumor. I guess you could say that we're mutants of sorts." Aiden slipped into his 'Doctor' voice, " Have you experienced any um, odd physical changes?"

Zoe suddenly looked frightened. "Like what?"

"Like if you're really angry or really scared...anything?"

"I'm really scared right now, and I haven't fucking changed since I was fucking twenty!!! What changes are you talking about? You think I have more of this shit to look forward too?!"

"No. No, I don't think so." Aiden patted Zoe's leg and resumed his pacing.

"You seem to have come to grips with all of this. How? How do you go out there and have a normal life?" Zoe needed to know how he'd accomplished what she failed so miserably at.

"My life isn't really very normal, honey, and I had um, guidance and the benefit of being told what I was at a very young age." Aiden moved towards the door.

Zoe pounced, blocking Aiden's exit. "You can't just leave me."

"I know. I'm not." He wiggled his cell phone in the air. "Just give me a minute. Okay?"

"Okay." Zoe held the door open for Aiden and closed it behind him.

Aiden needed to discuss this with Ian and called Kate, hoping she'd answer.

"Kate! I need to speak with Ian."

"Hello to you too. Here he is."

"Ian! Man, you won't fucking believe this -- you've got to help me out."

"Get yourself into another pickle?" Ian laughed.

"No! Fuck you! Well, yes, I did. Listen! Remember that girl I told you about?"

"Fucking shut up and listen to me! Claire, the redhead with the fiery temper. Remember? You thought she was good for me."

"Yeah, vaguely. That was a long time ago, she's got to be... "

"She's dead. She died a few years ago."

"Oh. I'm sorry, but I don't understand why you're so excited."

"Claire had a son; she named him Alexander. I saw his photo; he looks just like me."

"If he's yours, he's a Were."

"Was a Were. His woman shot him in the head and killed him, then killed herself."

"She knew what he was?"

"Probably. She had to have used a silver bullet to kill him. Why would you use silver unless you knew."

"Yeah, wow. So you had a son. I am sorry, that must ..."

"Wait. There's more. They had a daughter, Zoe.

My Granddaughter. I'm at her house now, and she's freaking out. She has no fucking clue except that she isn't aging, and her sense of smell and hearing...Oh fuck!" Aiden snapped his phone shut and leaped onto the porch and through the door.

Zoe was standing in the middle of the room, eyes bulging unfocused, tears running down her cheeks. She was able to hear every word Aiden had spoken.

"Zoe!" Aiden snapped his fingers in her face and patted her cheeks without effect. "Zoe, come on!" He pinched her arm and was immediately punched in the chest. Aiden stumbled backwards, coughing, impressed. "Okay. Okay." Aiden raised his hands in submission. "Great to have you back."

"What did you mean 'was a Were'? What's a Were? A Werewolf?"

"No. You must have misheard me."

Zoe threw another punch that Aiden intercepted. "Don't lie to me!"

"What the fuck am I supposed to tell you? That you're part I dunno, Cherokee and, hey by the way, part fucking Werewolf? "

"I am?"

"You see. And now you're going to fucking freak out, go all Wild Kingdom on my ass, scratch my eyes out. I don't have my med bag. If I was smart, I'd keep some Thorazine with me at all times; you just never fucking know when... "

Zoe started to giggle and then broke out into a genuine laugh. "You better chill Grandpa, or you'll have a Stoke."

"What?" It was Aiden's turn to be confused.

Zoe flopped back on the sofa, completely spent.

"This explains everything! It makes perfect sense. You have no idea what a relief this is."

Ian watched Zoe for a long while, he thought she'd fallen asleep she lay so quietly. Her voice startled him.

"I've never changed into anything. Not that I know of, anyway. Should I be able to?" Zoe opened her eyes and was looking across the room to Aiden.

"You'd definitely know if you'd ever changed. I don't know if you should be able to. I can't think of any other quarter Weres. I think you probably would have before you punched me in the chest, and any extreme emotions will do it too."

"Hmm. Now what?" Zoe felt like a child, ready to explore the world.

"You thought that you'd lost all of your family, as it turns out you have a rather large one. Would you like

to meet my cousin, your... I don't know what he would be to you."

"Yes, I would! Thanks Gramps!" Zoe pecked Aiden on the cheek.

"Don't! Please don't call me that." Aiden cringed.

"Let me get cleaned up. You know the house, I guess. Make yourself at home." Zoe ran up the stairs in twos.

***

I left Ian to potter in the kitchen and chat with Aiden.

The bathroom was filling with sweet lilac scented steam as I waited for the old clawfoot to fill.

I threw my robe on the chair and stepped in, almost too hot but not quite. I sank into the bubbles and gathered them around me. Perfect. Everything was perfect.

Ian opened the door and stepped into the clouds like a vision. "Mmmm, dessert? You look like a meringue."

"I feel like a creamy meringue."

I tucked my knees up as he stepped into the opposite end of the bath. I turned as he settled and laid my back against his chest. Ian let his hands roam over my body under the pretense of 'washing' me; they lingered on my breasts and between my legs. He was poking me in the back, and I did my best to distract myself. "What did Aiden want? He seemed a little upset."

"Yeah, remind me to tell you about that. Later. Turn around."

I did and found myself between his raised knees. He pushed his legs beneath the water and pulled me up onto his thighs wrapping my legs around his back. Ian kissed my lips, and teased me with his tongue, my own teasing back. He kissed along my neck and tenderly traced his bite mark with his tongue. I moaned, recalling that intense sensation. I reached between my legs, into the bubbles and found him hard and slick. My hand skimmed his length, the lightest touch, and twirled around his head, gliding over the top and back down. Our close proximity meant that I couldn't touch him without touching myself. I closed my eyes and enjoyed our mutual pleasure. Ian ensured that we remained pressed together by fondling my bottom. His fingers wandered down my crack and up as far as he could reach. Our fingers met during our activities and lingered for a moment, like a clandestine rendezvous. We smiled amidst a deep kiss. I loved the feeling of him in my hand, the restrained power. I wanted to taste him but couldn't see a way to achieve that in our current positions.

"Mmmm, yes. I think you'd drown, though." Ian had snuck into my thoughts.

"Later then?"

"I promise." Ian smiled.

We looked into each others' eyes; our thoughts were one. Ian grabbed my cheeks and lifted me as I positioned him at my entrance. Neither of us could check the speed of our movement; everything was too slippery. I slid onto him like a three-alarm fireman down a pole. I cried out but did not seek retreat. We could only manage slight shifts in our position. Wiggles and bumps. It was enough to raise the bath water into a stormy turmoil and enough to drive us into oblivion. We held each other as the water cooled around us. He slipped from my grasp, and I shivered.

"Come on. Out. You're going to catch a cold."

We dried ourselves and each other between kisses and intimate caresses and were well on our way to getting started again when my phone chirped and vibrated.

"Hello?"

"Kate, are you home?" It was Aiden.

"Yep, what's up?"

"Ian's there?"

"Yes. Do you need to speak with him?."

"No, just tell him we're coming over."

"He hung up." I snapped my phone shut. "Aiden said to tell you that they're coming over. Who?"

Ian rolled his eyes. "Aiden's a Grandfather. It's a long story. Better get dressed."

Chapter 3

Libby and Anna spent hours researching their mother's books, pouring over their fragile parchment and fading calligraphy. Her collection of paraphernalia and odds and sods was absolutely mind-boggling but thankfully well organized and cataloged. They'd gathered everything Libby would require, and she was keen to begin. Anna kissed her goodnight and left her alone in the attic room.

Libby stood beneath the window illuminated by the waning gibbous moon. She dropped her robe and, naked, basked in its silver glow. She smiled at the feeling of power growing within her. Everything was perfect, and her pulse was racing with excitement. It was time to begin.

Libby marked the room's four corners with lit candles; their flames flickered and swayed, casting a mesh of dancing shadows.

A large circle had been scribed in the center of the room by Libby's great grandmother and her sisters; though worn, it was still clearly visible. Libby walked around the circle three times, then stepped in and sat cross-legged on an old cushion in its center. Everything she required was spread out within the circle. She whispered an appropriate blessing and began.

Libby grasped a weighty, jeweled blade in her

right hand and drew a line across her left palm. She winced at the sting and centered the flow over an ornate ink well. The blood droplets ballooned and curled in the clear fluid in the vessel. She quickly dressed her wound and held the crystal well up to the moon light, giving it a swirl; the crimson turned an inky black.

Libby licked the nib of Raven's quill pen and dipped it into her ink. She smoothed a small square of parchment; it looked like the skin of an ancient and wrote in elaborate script -- Ian Alexander. The tail of the 'R' extended and enveloped the name in a heart; that ink returned to its original crimson red just as was described in her mother's book. Libby gently blew the ink dry and rolled the parchment, securing it with a delicate red ribbon.

Setting the parchment roll aside, Libby took a hand dipped candle Anna had found in one of their mother's many wooden boxes. They had wondered if their mother foresaw its use on this night. The candle was thick, long, and red, a roughly shaped phallus. She smiled, thinking of Ian. He would belong to her on the coming blue moon. His alpha power would be hers and the near immortality of a Were -- the thing she craved most.

Libby removed the bandage from her hand and tipped a vial of pungent smelling oil into her palm. It immediately reopened the wound, and small beads of blood rose from the red stripe and floated in the oil. She rubbed her hands together briskly, blending and warming the oil and blood until she thought her skin might burn with the heat. Libby grasped the red candle with both hands and began to caress its length. She closed her eyes and envisioned doing the same to Ian. She entwined his name in a chant of unworldly sounds, repeating it over and over as the candle warmed to her touch.

Libby opened a small Ziploc and retrieved three hairs she had stolen from Ian's head as she left him with Kate the other morning. She pressed them deep into the phallic candle and smoothed over the hollow, burying them within the soft wax.

Libby continued to sway, chant, and massage the candle deep into the night. Eventually, the flames at the four corners stuttered and died, leaving Libby in the grey light of pre-dawn.

Her hands were throbbing around the candle. It was as hot as her own skin yet no longer pliable; it was as rigid as stone. Libby's fingers glided over the candle's surface as though reading braille. Libby knew this candle was now the perfect likeness of a perfectly erect Ian. She smiled, "I am impressed, dear. This might turn out to be quite enjoyable."

Libby stood and stretched, grasping the light cord above her head. The illuminated vision of Ian's red candle in her hands filled her with lust and need. "Damn it! I can't risk everything on a little test drive; the real thing is going to be so much better." She gave the candle a kiss and carefully placed it in its box.

I unearthed some Assam tea I had tucked away for special occasions, and Ian approved. I thought of slipping him some Lipton to see if he could actually tell the difference. But trust is so delicate in a new relationship that I decided to keep the secret taste test for another day. We cuddled on the couch, sipping tea with Brubeck playing in the background.

"Aiden, a grandfather, that's just not right. I get that he's so much older than he looks, but a grandpa?" I shook my head.

"That he doesn't have any other children or grandchildren is infinitely more shocking."

"He's never found his other half?" An overwhelming sadness crept into my happy heart. "I always thought he was a lonely soul in spite of the constant entourage of girlies."

"He gave up the hunt many years ago. He met a Were in England, an older woman who somehow convinced him that she was his mate. Apparently, she was very convincing and had half of our family eating out of her hand." Ian frowned. "I was in Constantinople at the time but returned for the blue moon for their ceremony."

Ian's thoughts raced away, and I couldn't follow them.

When Ian spoke, I heard his thoughts as a sort of echo laced with emotions. When he was quiet, I felt his emotions like ripples or tsunamis, unless he 'spoke' in his mind. Sometimes there was nothing. I assumed that he could close his mind's door and keep me out.

He was quiet for a while, and something about him looked very old or pained. I touched his hand, and he returned to me.

"As it happens, what she really wanted was the next Alpha. She thought it was Aid, and he was while I was away. I arrived during the ceremony and joined everyone in my wolf form.

She could tell that I was the successor to alpha

by the way my family greeted me. She slinked over to me and gave me her underside and neck -- without a glance back to Aiden, right in the middle of their ceremony. She left him for me, for the Alpha rather. It crushed him, destroyed a part of him. He left ran off into the woods. He wandered through Europe and didn't come back to England for years."

"What did you do?" I asked carefully.

"I tore her throat out."

The rumble of Aiden's bike rescued our thoughts, returning them to the present day. Ian raised his brows, "this should be interesting."

"This is Zoe, my granddaughter." Aiden beamed with a mixture of pride and awkwardness. "Zoe, Kate, and Ian my cousin." Aiden completed the introductions.

Zoe gave me a flicker of a smile. The smile she gave Ian was absolutely blinding. I placed my hand in Ian's, but she didn't seem to notice.

"You look nothing like Aiden, thank God! Ian elbowed his cousin.

"I don't know, I think we have the same lips." Zoe licked her lips.

"Hmmm," Ian was studying the similarities.

Yeah, they're manly.

Ian snorted at my thoughts and squeezed my hand.

Zoe barely noticed that I was in the room or that Ian and I were obviously together. She touched Ian's arm as she spoke, "So, you're a werewolf, too. I want to learn more about us, about you. Everything." She glanced at me to ensure that I felt excluded.

My blood was beginning to boil.

Aiden giggled and grabbed my arm, pulling me into the kitchen. "Shall we make some of those charming cucumber sandwiches you're so fond of? Kate?!" He dragged me away.

"Come on." He turned on the kitchen radio and raised the volume, laughing all the while.

"What are you doing?" I was puzzled and annoyed. I needed to get back to guarding Ian.

"You're so fucking hysterical!" Aiden spoke in a laughing whisper. "Jealousy doesn't suit you, Kate."

"I'm not jealous!" Was it that obvious?

"Get used to it, honey. He's an Alpha, and the girls all want a piece of it."

I was about to give Aiden a piece of my jealous wrath, but a feeling of woe collapsed onto my shoulders. I might be able to fight off Zoe, but all of the female kind?

I was close to tears. "Aiden, what can I do? I love him."

Aiden pulled me into a hug. "I know you do." He kissed the top of my head and held me for a long while. "He loves you too. You're the one."

I stepped back from Aiden; his sad eyes contradicted his smile. I wished I could help him heal.

"So, you're a grandfather."

"Yeah. Unfuckingbelievable."

We returned to the living room empty-handed. Ian and Zoe were sat on the sofa chatting. Ian stood, displacing her hand from his leg. Aiden chuckled and shook his head.

Ian's eyes crinkled with his smile. He wrapped his arms around me and kissed me possessively.

There, now she knows. You're the only one for me, Kate.

You could have let her know earlier.

That might have seemed rude, but you were both very entertaining.

I jabbed Ian in the ribs, and he laughed. The tension in the room quickly dissipated, along with my jealousy. Zoe scooted to the end of the sofa, allowing Ian and I to sit together. Aiden left for the kitchen and returned with a tray of cookies and four glasses of lemonade.

I noticed the red specks of cayenne pepper in the drinks. "That's Libby's cleansing lemonade. I don't know if we should..."

"I know. It's what she always serves me. I like it -- it's got a kick. Slainte!" Aiden held his glass in the air and then emptied it.

Zoe took a cautious sip. "I think I read about this, isn't it what Beyonce drinks? It can't be all that bad; look at her."

"Beyonce?" I looked at Aiden. "I don't think Lib's mixture is strong enough, or maybe you're just immune to its effects?" Ian caught the cushion Aiden hurled at me. Aiden was nearly as gorgeous as Ian, but I doubted it had anything to do with a lemonade cleanse.

We were all curious about Zoe. She skimmed over her "unremarkable youth" and what she remembered of her parents' life and death. "My parents were only 19 when they had me, and I was 5 when they...died. Gran raised me. She was the most loving and generous person I've ever known. I miss her."

I squeezed Zoe's hand, and she continued. "I've always loved running. Any sort of running, sprints, distance, I guess I understand why now. I got a track scholarship to Stanford. I hated leaving Gran, but she insisted. That's about the time I began to notice my senses becoming more acute. It scared the shit out of me." Zoe looked at Aiden. "I really thought I had a brain tumor."

"Heightened senses? That could be handy." I could think of a few uses.

"Right? But kinda hard to enjoy when you're convinced your brain is cancerous cauliflower. That wasn't the extent of my freakiness either. I excelled in track, really excelled, attracting all sorts of unwanted attention. And I beat up a guy for touching my ass, pulverized him. You can imagine what that did for my popularity. After that, I kept to myself, finished my degree, and came home. Gran made me join various clubs and tried to get me to socialize." Zoe shook her head, "I knew I was different; people inevitably saw it, too. Nothing lasted. I stopped trying after Gran died; I quit trying to look my age. I worked from home, rarely left my house, and experienced the world through TV and tabloids."

"Then I came along and rescued you!" Aiden piped in.

"You came along looking for some ass!" Zoe threw the stray cushion back at Aiden.

"Sniffing around your own granddaughter -- you're one sick puppy, Aid." Ian shook his head.

"I'm staying away from her ass; she'd pulverize me too."

"That's probably all that's stopping you!" Ian

accused playfully.

"Right?" Zoe and I nodded at each other.

The three of them looked towards the front door long before I heard clamoring and bitching. Libby. Aiden opened the door for her.

"Hello, children! Mummy's home. Have you behaved yourselves?"

Aiden reached for her large shoulder bag, and Libby slapped his hand away and clutched it to her. She stepped back from the doorway and indicated the red pile at the base of the drive.

"And I thought sea air was supposed to work wonders on one's constitution...you're still a bitch." Aiden grumbled and leaped down the steps.

"And who is this?" Libby clicked over in her Louboutin spikes and extended her hand to Zoe.

"Hi, I'm Zoe. Aiden's...." She looked from me to Ian.

"Sister. Half sister. My half cousin." Ian filled in.

Libby raised her brow but didn't comment. "Well, pleased to meet you, Zoe." Libby spotted the glasses. "Aiden!!!" I was amazed she could move so quickly on those heels. She opened the front door as Aiden stepped in sideways with her luggage. "You drank all of my lemonade again?! Damn it Aid!"

Aiden unceremoniously dumped Lib's bags in the middle of the entry. "Yea, it was delish. But you know, now that I see you again, I think they're right."

"What?"

"You must have screwed up the recipe. You look nothing like Beyonce either. She has perfect glowing skin -- you're too pale. I hear she's a very pleasant person, whereas you... and she has a perfect ass."

Aiden spun Libby around for a look. "Well, my ass is perfect, yours... "

Libby slapped the side of Aiden's head, "You should stick to what you know Aid, and you'll never know this." She patted her bum and began to drag her luggage into her room. Aiden gave in and helped.

Libby excused herself to unpack and take a nap.

The four of us talked and joked. Aiden gave us a spot-on impression of Libby, perky breasts and all. He had us in hysterics. I never could figure those two out. Libby always called Aiden if she needed anything, and Aiden was always there to help her out. Yet they seemed to have an intense dislike for each other.

Zoe and I got on as though we'd known each other forever. I was quite pleased that I didn't follow my first instinct to throttle her.

"I'm starving; anyone else?" Ian got up and stretched. "Anywhere to eat in this town?"

"Sonny Williams' Steak Room." Aiden and I suggested in chorus.

"Sounds utterly perfect. Okay with you, Zoe?"

"I've heard of it; I think you need reservations."

"Others do. We don't. The owner and I are tight." Aiden boasted.

"That's my grand dad!!"

"What did I say about calling me that? Do I have to spank you?"

Zoe raised her eyebrows in a challenge.

"You think you could take me on a little girl?"

"I'd whoop your ass, old man!" They wrestled playfully for a moment. Zoe had some impressive moves; I could easily imagine her "pulverizing" a normal guy.

"Hey, shouldn't we ask Libby if she wants to come?" Zoe asked, a little out of breath.

"No!!" I shrieked.

"God, no! Libby's a witch if you disturb her beauty, rest," Aiden warned.

Ian herded everyone out.

Zoe stopped at Aiden's bike. "Hey, can I take her for a ride?"

"No fucking way. No one rides Sheila E but me."

"What do you call your Jeep?" Ian asked with trepidation.

"Um...Jeep?"

Ian opened the passenger door for me, and I dropped the keys into his waiting hand without hesitation. He slid into the driver's side and bashed his knees before adjusting the seat. Everything about us felt right about Ian, but the suddenness of it all left me feeling a little dazed, as though I'd wake up to my real life any minute.

Ian pinched my leg, and I jumped. "You are awake. This is your real life".

Libby woke from her nap refreshed and to a blissfully silent house. She showered, dressed in a short, clingy floral dress, and inspected her curves in her full-length mirror. "Baby, you've got it, and it won't be long before he wants it."

"Now, Kate, what are we going to do about you?" Libby pulled a shopping list of items to be collected, things that were intimately Kate. She placed an empty shoebox on Kate's dresser and began checking off items as she placed them in the box. She gathered hair from her brush, snipped a sample of cloth from the inside hems of Kate's favorite clothes, and dabbed Kate's favorite perfume on the samples. Libby pulled a photo album down from a shelf and browsed through its pages. "What does he see in you?" Libby began to burn with jealousy as her eyes flicked from image to image. She pulled a photo from its sleeve and dropped it with the other things into the box.

Libby secured the shoebox lid with a ribbon. She sat on Kate's bed for a moment and closed her eyes. The room was filled with Ian's scent and the unmistakable smell of sex. Images of Kate and Ian's glistening bodies writhing together exploded in Libby's mind, filling her with anger and lust.

Libby learned to control her anger reasonably well long ago; gaining control of her sexual desires was another thing entirely.

She lay back on Kate's bed and breathed deep of Ian's scent, ignoring Kate's. "Ian. I want you. I need your powerful wolf." Libby reached between her legs and pushed the flimsy fabric of her thong to one side. Her nails grazed her lips, and her fingers plunged, stirring her juices. She rubbed herself frantically, racing towards release. She imagined Ian deep inside of her, stretching her with his wolven knot. Her back arched, and her legs spasmed as she came. The intensity surprised her. "God, Ian, I can't wait to have you in more than just my imagination!"

Libby stretched and wiggled her red enameled toes. "Back to work; the sooner we get her out of the way, the better." She hopped off the bed, grabbed the box, and left for her rented loft in the city.

Once there, Libby cheerfully constructed Kate's

demise.

We drove home from Sonny's in a gluttonous stupor. Actually, I was the only one in a stupor; the others were animated in their conversation, telling Zoe old timey stories. Embarrassing moments caught naked after a 'change', no clothes in sight, being chased by poachers, the stories seemed endless.

"Hey, let's stop for a pint!" Aiden interrupted my thoughts of climbing into my comfy bed and sleeping.

"Ugh, Aiden, I'm tired, I don't have your mad metabolism."

"Come on, Kate, for Zoe! It's like her 'coming out' night."

"Okay, okay. Maybe Ken'll make me a coffee."

It was so strange to be back at our local. It seemed a lifetime ago that Ian and I had met here when in reality, only a few days had passed.

We walked through the door, and all eyes turned towards us. Aiden waved away my favorite beer as it appeared on the counter. "She needs some coffee."

Ken left and returned with a steamy cup. "Cream, no sugar, right Kate?"

"You're the best." The coffee was perfect, indeed, just what I needed.

A cute guy immediately approached Zoe, she looked happy. Swarms of females buzzed around Ian and Aid as they tried to order their drinks.

Ken looked from the girls and Ian to me. "Are you okay Kate?"

"Yes, very okay. Happy. I mean...yes, I am."

Ken raised his brows and smiled, "Well, alright then."

Ian joined me sporting a thin white mustache. I pulled him down to me a kissed it away. Ian returned the kiss, and we found ourselves drifting towards the door.

"Is it always going to be like this? A simple kiss, and we catch on fire?" I asked.

Before Ian could answer, glass shattered towards the back of the bar. I caught glimpses of a broken beer bottle being waved in the air, punctuating angry slurs.

Ian held me behind him as people quickly vacated the bar. A frightened Zoe joined us and held my hand.

As the room cleared, it became apparent that a bulky football type was threatening a rather beautiful 'metro-male' with a broken beer bottle.

Aiden was lounging in a chair nearby giggling. The slender guy didn't appear at all worried by the drunken hulk. In fact he was laughing as well.

Our bouncer ushered a few more people out, and I caught him pointing to me while looking at Ken. Ken shook his head, and the bouncer locked the bar doors.

I didn't know what was going on; the entire scene was surreal. The atmosphere of the bar had changed, it was supercharged and seemed more and more like a Quentin Tarantino film and less like the local I was used to.

Ian growled, and his skin tingled where it was touching mine. Only a few people remained in the bar. They were all beautiful with perfect bone structure, though quite pale. Ken and the bouncer too. How odd that I'd never noticed before.

The hulk was growing angrier as his abuse seemed only to humor the 'metro male'.

"Keep your fucking hands off my woman, or I'll break your pretty little neck!"

"Now, now. She's far too sweet for you and intelligent -- she prefers me."

The hulk lunged and was immediately pounced on by several bystanders.

Aiden's chair was knocked off balance landing him on his ass.

He finally stopped giggling. "Okay, that's enough. I'm not on call tonight, but they always manage to find me to help clean up blood and gore, and I'm not in the mood. Get the fuck out, take your skinny bitch with you."

Hulk and the skinny bitch looked scared shitless and couldn't get out fast enough.

"Wow, Aiden, you rock!" Zoe shouted from behind Ian and the rest of the room turned towards her voice, their elongated, pointed teeth barely concealed.

Aiden started giggling again, but it sounded far away, like in a tunnel. I felt prickles all over my skin, the room began to spin, and I was overcome by the need to sleep. Huh, vampires. That's so funny.

Ian was calling my name from miles away. I could no longer feel my body, no longer hear their calls. I fell into a grey, consuming fog.

Chapter 4

Libby arrived at her rented city loft and breathed deep of the herbs and other scents that only a witch would be able to identify. She poured herself a glass of Clos Du Mesnil and popped a Mazzy Star disc on. Libby danced and swayed around the large room, collecting items from shelves as she circled.

She placed her ingredients and the contents of the shoe box on a large, ornate table in the center of the room. Everything she needed was here; did she really have to wait for Anna? She decanted another flute and watched the tiny bubbles rise in their graceful columns - marching along like moments in time.

"Damn it Anna! I can't just stand around waiting. Besides, I don't need your help with this".

Libby gulped the entire glass of bubbles, visualizing their panic and giggling at their foiled attempt at escape. She focused on the enjoyable task ahead.

"Sugar and spice and everything nice or snips of snails and rattlesnake tails, let's see what our Kate is made of".

Libby made a cross with two willow sticks and twine. She padded the sticks with Spanish moss and continued wrapping the thread around while whispering an incantation. She added the trimmed photo of Kate to the layers of twine, then covered it in a head-to-toe bandage of cotton ribbon. The sticks now resembled a crude doll.

Libby sewed the pieces of Kate's clothing to the doll, threaded Kate's hair into the top of the doll's head and secured two brown glass beads for eyes. "There, looks just like you!" She imagined jabbing the sewing needle between the glass beads but stabbed the pin cushion instead. An opposing pin stuck her finger tip and Libby jumped back with a shriek "you little bitch! Laugh while you can..." the doll's simple expression remained unchanged. Libby licked the red pearl from her finger, glaring at Kate's likeness.

"This," Libby angrily tapped a large mason jar with her nail, "...is going to be your new home. What do you think? Cozy, huh?"

Libby gathered a list of items and threw them into a large mortar. "A pinch of dried hibernating bear blood - yum! Valerian, Jamaica Dogwood, Poppy, St John's wort, Skullcap..." she continued with a few more obscure ingredients, then furiously ground them into a fine dust.

Libby collected the powder on a damp wad of Kapok fiber, stuffed it into the Mason jar, and quickly secured the lid. She washed her hands and the mortar and pestle and returned to the table.

Libby poured another glass and drank it absent mindedly. She held the empty crystal up to the light and watched the chips of rainbow dance around the table. She caught a glint in the doll's glass eyes and felt strangely threatened. She couldn't wait for Anna's arrival. Libby quickly opened the jar, dropped 'Kate' in and secured the lid, breathing a sigh of relief.

Libby gave the jar a little shake. The dolls bead eyes clinked against the glass. Libby finished the bottle of wine and fell asleep at the table under the doll's captivated gaze.

⸺⸻◇⸻⸺

Ian caught Kate as she collapsed. "Kate! Kate!! Jesus Aiden! I can't believe you would take her here! Ian glared at the vampires surrounding them. The only thing keeping him from changing into his wolf was the need to help Kate. Zoe stood by them in an attack pose, ready to pounce.

"Jesus Christ! Will you all just fucking relax?! These are my friends. Kate's safer here than anywhere out there! She's just fainted."

"Yeah? She's not coming to. Kate! Wake up!!" Ian gently shook Kate's shoulders, but she didn't respond. "Kate!!"

"Ian! Calm down! Let me see her." Aiden pushed Ian out of his way.

Aiden checked Kate's pulse. It was slow and strong. Her pupils were equal and reacted briskly to light. Her breathing was unlabored. He made a fist and firmly pressed his knuckles into Kate's sternum. Nothing. Aiden removed her sandals and ran his thumbnail along her soul from heel to toe - nothing happened.

"What! What does that mean?" Ian demanded.

"That," Aiden indicated Kate's foot, "...was good. But she isn't responding to painful stimuli; that's not so good. Ken, get us an ambulance."

Ian discreetly slipped Kate's blouse from her shoulder, revealing the bite mark to Aiden.

"Get one of our ambulances," Aiden instructed. Ken redialed.

Ian was beside himself with worry and guilt. Aiden grasped his shoulder. "You didn't do this. This isn't what happened to our Great Gran. Ian, keep it together, man".

The ambulance arrived in no time. Its crew, a male and female jumped out giving Aiden a quick nod. They were

beautiful, like opals set in black jumpsuits. They deftly placed Kate on a stretcher and lifted her into their van.

Ian moved to climb in, but Aiden pushed him aside. "This is my territory; let me do what I do best. Follow with Zoe."

Ian growled and sprinted to Kate's Jeep, barely waiting for Zoe.

Aiden called the ED and cleared a trauma room. He ordered an MRI and labs and had Neuro stand by. His personal ED team met them as they backed into the Ambulance dock. The crew gave a quick and thorough handover and left. Aiden and the team rushed Kate's stretcher into the trauma room and closed the doors. They immediately began to take vitals, draw blood, connect Kate to a cardiac monitor, and start an IV.

Jillian, Aiden's most trusted RN reviewed results as they presented. "Everything's coming back normal Aid, is there any relevant family history, trauma, anything?"

Aiden slid the hospital gown from Kate's shoulder.

Jillian nodded. "Yours?"

"No." Aiden's tone had a hint of regret.

"Hmm, well, I've never seen a 'dog' bite induced coma, not without sepsis."

"She's not septic." Aiden said shaking his head. "Get her up to radiology, we need that MRI."

Ian pushed through the entrance doors as Kate was being wheeled to the elevator.

"We haven't found anything yet, we're taking her up for an MRI. Ian, I'll find out what's going on with her. Keep cool." Aiden looked into Ian's eyes until his words sunk in. He knew Ian was on the verge of an uncontrolled shift.

Ian nodded, taking a deep breath and touching Kate's peaceful face.

The elevator dinged and they piled in around the stretcher.

"Jillian", Aiden barked "...get Libby Blackhouse; she works on Ortho. She might be able to help."

Aiden's cell phone vibrates as they wheel out of the elevator. "Yes?"

"Apparently, Libby didn't show up for work tonight," Jillian reported.

"What? I thought...never mind. Get me a bed on Neuro."

Ian insisted on spending the night at Kate's bedside. It passed in a blur of white coats and clinical voices and seemed unending. The reluctant morning sun shone orange through the white blinds, and daylight softened the features of the sleep deprived. Kate remained unchanged, though now her life was reflected and encouraged by a plethora of monitors, drips, and tubes.

"Aid?" Libby stepped into Kate's room with coffee and bagged breakfasts from the cafeteria. "I came as soon as I heard. What happened?"

"Where were you?!" Aiden snapped.

Libby took a nervous step backward. "Working."

"Really?! We looked for you. I have some questions."

Libby was used to arguing with doctors and lying. She swallowed and stepped into her role. "I was pulled to Ortho! What questions?!" She braced herself for an accusation.

"Has Kate been acting strange lately?"

"What?" Libby's shoulders relaxed. "Kate always acts..." Libby bit her tongue. "No, not unusually strange."

Aiden was too tired to be patient or to humor. His tone was clipped and chilled, "Libby, has Kate fallen recently, complained of dizziness, headaches, eaten anything unusual, complained of anything? Anything at all?"

Libby let her breath out, relieved. "No. No, she hasn't. Not to me. What happened?"

Aiden gave Libby a heavily edited version of events.

Libby had to work hard to conceal her delight. "Oh my God." Her voice cracked with the effort and was misinterpreted as genuine concern. It worked! I did it!!

Kate's mind drifted through dreams. Odd dreams filled with disturbing images and scents of strange voices speaking strange languages. She had flashes

of Hollywood vampires and hairy beasts and then of
Ian.- the other half of her two-piece puzzle. Click - a
perfect fit. She loved everything about him, about
Ian the man. Ian the wolf - she wasn't so sure about.

Her mind floated off and landed in a Piggly
Wiggly market, pushing around a giant cart of
vacuum packed meat . Finding that thought
somewhat unpleasant her mind immediately
transformed the cart full of carcass

into a cart full of a very juicy looking Ian. He had
a barcode on his forehead and the sell-by date had
been erased. Kate giggled but it came out as the
tinkle of piano keys.

The cart became Aiden's Harley in the blink of a
dreamy eye. Two figures were poised on its seat,
clinging to each other as if speeding away. Aiden
and one of his girlies Kate supposed. But just as that
thought formed the larger person in front removed
his black helmet - it was Ian. His face was beautiful,
his eyes gleamed darkly with passion and his lips
were so inviting. Kate stepped towards the bike,
longing to taste Ian's lips. Before she could reach out
to him, the passenger removed her helmet - it was
Libby! Libby smiled, with her arms wound around
Ian like a Boa Constrictor.

The image of the perfect two-piece puzzle
returned. Upon closer inspection, Kate realized that
the pieces had been forced together- not a perfect
match. The image was shattered, curled up at the
edges, and frightening.

Kate screamed soundlessly. Ian!!! She was
floating in the grey, swirling fog like a tuft of down.
Is this a dream? Am I dreaming of being trapped in

a dream?? I just have to relax. Just roll over and wake up. Wake up!! Damn it, wake up!!! Am I dead?

Kate tried to recall the events of the evening, half expecting to see herself mangled in a terrible car crash or shot by a drug-seeking ER patient or...vampires. Kate focused her attention on her body. I don't feel sore or bitten, I don't feel DEAD! Her mind was quiet for a moment, exhausted.

Voices began to drift into her consciousness. Familiar voices that made her want to cry with joy.

It was Aiden. "I don't want to move her! I don't think she should fly!! What if..."

"What exactly are we doing for her here?! She's wasting away! God damn it Aiden, I can't just stand by and watch her d..." Ian's voice faded.

Ian, I'm here. Please hear me! Why can't you hear my thoughts?

"Her parents have asked me to fly her home. I know people in London, you know people there, specialists," Ian continued.

"Jesus Christ! I've fucking called in every favor and discussed this with every specialist out there. What the fuck do you think I've been doing for the past four months?!"

Four months. How is that even possible? What's wrong with me? What happened? Kate listened beyond their silence. Familiar sounds - a hospital room. The steady beep of an IV pump and of a cardiac monitor. I don't appear to be on a vent, that's good. Right?

"Come on, boys, this isn't helping." It was Libby. "Ian honey, let's go home. We'll be able to think clearer with a little sleep under our belts. Come on babe." Her voice was dripping with sickly sweetness. Kate was overcome with anger and hurt; she knew that tone - Libby's tone of ownership. Kate felt her heart twisting painfully in her chest.

"You go, I'm going to stay for a while," Ian spoke quietly.

"Honey, you really need..."

"Don't! Please, just go. Please. Aid will walk you to your car."

"I don't need Aiden to walk me to my car. Fine. I'll see you in the morning." Libby bent to kiss Ian and left

"The family will all be together for the blue moon. If we brought Kate to them, to the stones, maybe that power, that energy would help bring her back. I have to do something, Aid."

"My friends have suggested...they've suggested changing her." Aiden took a step back from Ian as he spoke. "I don't want to lose her either. I'd prefer Kate the vampire over no Kate at all."

Ian jumped to his feet and grabbed a fistful of labcoat. "Let any of those leeches near her, and I'll break their necks - and yours!" Ian slammed Aiden against the wall.

Aiden understood his anger. "Okay. Okay. We'll make arrangements for transport to The Royal. I suppose that it's about time I returned to London, face the family."

Aiden turned Kate's music on to instill some life into the room, then left unnoticed.

Ian let his great sadness collapse across his face, his being. He couldn't be strong for her. He couldn't hide behind that expansive wall when they were alone. They were without boundary, without barrier, a single soul.

He replaced the solitary Iris in its tall crystal vase at Kate's bedside - Libby would move it to an unseen corner daily. Ian's fingers lingered along the flower's violent purple curls, and memories crashed into his undefended mind, destroying him yet again. Beautiful images deliver exquisite pain. He sank into a chair by her side and held her hand between his; its stillness startled him even now.

"I'm here, Kate." His tears traced tired lines unnoticed. He held her fingers to his lips and closed his burning eyes. They were ghosts bound to one another in limbo, unable to save themselves or each other.

Kate's favorite CD played in the background, so familiar that it became part of the silence. 'Desert' began to play, an acoustic, haunting version - not the one that he'd watch transform her. Ian strained to listen and translated the French in a whisper and with effort.

The words invaded him, wound around his pain, defining it, lighting the darkness, and making it deeper.

"Oh my love, my soul mate
I count the days I count the hours
I'd like to place you in a desert
The desert of my heart.
Oh, my love, the grain of your voice made me happy at every step.

Let me place you in a desert, the desert of my
heart
  In night, I sometimes put my nose to the window
  I'm waiting and dark in a desert, in my desert.
  There.
  Oh, my love, my heart is heavy I count the hours
I count the days I'd like to place you in a desert
  The desert of my heart
  Oh, my love, I gave up my turn
  I deserted those around me
  I'm leaving you. There. That's all
  In the night I sometimes put my nose to the
window
  I'm waiting, and dark
  Wind, take my sad ash. There."
  Ian's voice crumbled as he spoke the last few
words. He collapsed, burying his face against her
tummy, and wept into her covers, wrenching sobs
that shook against her stillness. His heart fell apart
and blew away like desert sand.
  Ian quieted and remained folded over her, as still
as she. Darkness had crept into the room. Ian turned
her bedside lamp on and lifted himself from her,
feeling heavy with the emptiness. "I love you." His
lips caressed her ear as he spoke. Each word
burdened with despair.
  "I have to return to England..." his features
distorted with pain. He kissed her lips, laid her hand
at her side, and walked out.
  A tear welled in Kate's lashes and rolled down
her cheek, unseen.
  "You have to keep the jar near Kate, at least in
the same town, or it'll lose its effect." Anna did not

share in Libby's enthusiasm for this project. "Don't you think you should consider letting go Lib? It doesn't seem to be going as you'd hoped."

"It's going exactly as planned. " Libby countered. "He'll be eating his little dog biscuits out of my hand in no time at all. Are you sure that you won't come to England with me? I'd like you to be there when it happens."

"Please rethink this, Lib" Anna pleaded, "You won't have your powers to back you up on that night, not within the Stones. It, Ian, will see you for who you are, what you are. I just don't want...I don't want anything bad to happen to you."

"Nothing bad will happen, just a little eternal love bite. We'll be leaving next week..." Libby looked hopefully at her sister, who shook her head. "Well, I'll call you from London, think about it. Okay?"

⸺⸺◦⸺⸺

Aiden found returning to his old hospital a painful challenge; it had been many years since he had worked there. He saw familiar faces hiding beneath the misty veil of age, young girls full of energy and enthusiasm now in the winter of their lives -- matronly ward Sisters, nurses, doctors. He caught a few of them taking long looks, studying his face, trying to make sense of the emotions stirred by this young man. One approached him, lightly touching his arm, "You look so much like a boy I, um...knew." The painful crumbling of her heart could be heard in each word. Aiden smiled softly and patted her hand until she let it fall from his arm

I remember you too Becky. I'm sorry for causing you any pain. Aiden looked with sudden clarity into her sad, tired eyes. I'm so sorry for breaking your heart. Becky struggled with a smile, turned, and walked away.

"My life is such a fucking trail of tragedies," Aiden mumbled to himself, his unhappiness taking root.

Ian's family began preparations for the Blue Moon, for the transfer of power from Ian's father to Ian. For a brief time, while with Kate, Ian felt like the Alpha, but now? He didn't have the energy or interest. He felt himself fading away, being dragged under, and no more so than when he was with Libby. Her pull on him was nauseating and beyond his comprehension. She clung to him, smothering and confusing him, clouding his vision.

Ian found solace at Kate's side, speaking softly in her ear, holding her hand. He had insisted that Kate was discharged to his family home from the Royal. Aiden had a handpicked medical team in house 24/7, and Kate's family couldn't have hoped for better care for her.

"Libby plans on being at the ceremony next week; you know that, don't you?" Aiden frowned; his distaste for her had become palpable over the past few months.

"I couldn't give a fat fuck what she does." Ian grimaced, "I'm starting to sound like you."

"You've been hanging around her too much."

Ian's features boiled with instant fury.

"Libby! I meant Libby. Relax! Libby's a fucking witch!." Aiden shot a glance at Ian; something in his words rang true. "Do you think...could she actually be a witch?"

"I've never caught that scent on her Aid. I don't want to talk about her anymore and I don't care if she comes or not, I don't really want to be there myself."

"I know, man, but the family..."

"Yea, yea." Ian turned to leave the room as Libby entered and collided with his chest. Ian reached out to steady her, and the fuzzy cloud descended. He held her for a moment, unable to let go.

Libby looked coldly from Aiden and smiled sweetly up at Ian. "Honey, I've been looking for you everywhere in your big old house. Been hiding from me?"

"No. I was just..." Ian looked over to his sleeping soul mate, a therapist was stretching her limbs and massaging her muscles.

"Of course. Silly me." Libby's voice dripped with sarcasm, cutting through Ian's thoughts.

Aiden pushed past Libby but not before taking a few sniffs that gave him no information at all beyond what he had long known -- Libby wore very expensive perfume. They scowled at each other and Aiden marched off, pulling Ian with him.

Libby moved to Kate's bedside seething with anger "Get out!" she yelled at the therapist. The uniformed muscles paused, unsure of Libby's status in the house.

Libby raised her brows in a challenge and the therapist left.

Libby flipped her phone open and dialed Anna's number but was only able to leave a message. "Damn it Anna, call me as soon as you get this. I overheard Ian and Aid speaking of witches. I don't know if they're catching on, if Aiden thinks he knows something, nosy bastard. Ian is completely in the dark. Call me, I need you to be here."

Libby was annoyed with her sister, with Aiden and with Ian, she wanted to hurt something. She leaned over Kate and whispered into her ear, "I suppose you've heard Ian and I will be mated in just a few days, on the blue moon. It's going to be so beautiful". Libby touched Kate's lower lip, her blood-red enamel a stark contrast to Kate's pale tone. "Whatever made you think that he would want to be with you? That he would choose you over me? You have nothing to offer him. Nothing."

—•—

Aiden couldn't stop thinking of Libby being an actual witch. It seemed to make all of the pieces fit into place, Kate's sudden and inexplicable collapse, her strangle hold on Ian, and the one she used to have on him. He made a few calls. "Victor? It's me, Aid. Do me a huge favor. There's a girl staying with us, Libby Blackhouse. Check her out for me. Yeah, she may not be playing straight. Thanks, man." A few more calls like that, and he felt he had enough feelers out into all levels of existence. He studied Ian, crumpled in a leather wingback, twitching in his uneasy sleep. Next to him, completely still lay Kate, the horrid tube in her nose looking like a gash of spray paint across la Giaconda. They were both perched on death's edge, waiting for the other to jump.

"Thank God you came!" Libby picked Anna up from Heathrow. "Aid has his little fanged puppets out asking questions, I can't keep my eyes on everyone -- Thank you for helping me!"

"I didn't say I would help. I'm here to try to convince you to let this go. It's too dangerous Lib, you're crazed, obsessed with this, and you're not thinking clearly. Please..." Anna pleaded.

"No! You're wrong and if you're not going to help me then you can march yourself right back on that plane!" Libby stabbed her finger back towards the gates.

"Geeze Lib. You're my sister, I'll help. I'll do what I can." They both knew the conversation would end this way.

Libby hugged her twin, "You see, everything will be just fine! This is what you need to do... "

That night Anna drove to Ian's home determined to do her best to make everyone think she'd been there a dozen times before. Libby's orders were to keep Aiden busy and out of her hair, and her advice -"Just be a bitch; he'll never know that you're not me." Anna had studied photographs of the family and hoped she'd get them straight when it counted. "Just call 'em all 'honey', you can't go wrong".

Anna felt a strange pang when she was shown the photo of Aiden. He was handsome, she thought, but that didn't account for the tingle in her spine.

A uniformed man let Anna in, swiftly stepping

aside as she ignored him and pushed through, disguising her anxiety with Libby-like brusqueness.

Now where? Anna closed her eyes for a moment and envisioned the map of the house Libby had drawn. Up to my room... to hide. She climbed the central staircase, head down, hoping to go unnoticed. Right at the top and ... she ran smack into Aiden.

Aiden grabbed her arms to save her from a neck breaking topple back down the stairs. "What the fuck Libby! Better watch where you're going or you might have a nasty little..." Aiden looked into Anna's eyes and couldn't finish his sentence or think of what he might have been trying to say. "Fuck", was all that came out.

Aiden shook his head, cautiously moved Anna away from him, and let go of her. "Fuck." He squinted at her, and then his eyes widened "I'm right, you are a fucking witch! What, you're finally realizing that Ian doesn't want you, and now you're going to sprinkle some twinkly dust on me? You're not my other half, not my soul mate! How the bloody Hell are you pulling this one off? I ought to break your fucking neck!" Aiden took a breath to continue but had that same breath knocked out of him before he could open his mouth.

Please stop, please! Stop yelling at me, I haven't done anything to you Anna was whimpering in her head and Aiden was hearing every word as though spoken. This was something that only true mates had; he didn't think it could be conjured up with hocus pocus.

Anna was on the edge of tears. Aiden touched

her face, and she felt that electric bolt in her spine once again. Aiden was a cyclone of confusion, how all of a sudden is this bitch my soul mate? "Libby, I don't know how you're doing this, but let me tell you, you are treading on very dangerous ground." Aiden's eyes blazed with passion.

I'm not Libby.

"What!?" Aiden's gentle touch on Anna's arm tightened painfully.

"I'm not Libby," Anna looked pained and defeated. "I'm her sister Anna." Aiden twisted his head, looking very much like a puzzled puppy. "We're twins, identical twins."

"I didn't know she had a twin sister." Aiden looked into Anna's eyes once again and felt his heart swirling like an eddy of molten lava. The liquid rock flowed through him and solidified painfully in the front of his trousers.

Anna felt it, too. Her central furnace lit and was sending waves of heat through her body. Their thoughts had become exclusive; nothing and no one else existed.

Aiden lightly held Anna's hand and stepped backward towards his room, she followed, maintaining the light touch.

Aiden had spent much of his childhood in this room. The decor had changed many times over the centuries, but it continued to be dark and heavy, wreaked of manly emotion and cedar. The blood red silks and brocade, the cloudlike down bedding and pillows -¬they scared him, speaking a language that he could not begin to understand, until this moment. The afternoon sun shone through the wall of windows and caught silver and crystal, sending twinkles of light to all corners.

Aiden bent to kiss Anna; her lips were burning and parted in a 'welcome home'. His steel-clad heart clicked open and absorbed the love and passion in his surroundings. At last. He could have sobbed with the relief, with the overwhelming emotion of it all, but Anna's tongue had met his, and her hands were in his hair, pulling him to her.

Clothes were shed in a way that appeared choreographed and in slow motion. They barely touched as garments pooled on the polished hardwood beneath their feet. Once they were completely naked they stood utterly still for a moment, admiring each other, letting their eyes wander. Aiden gently guided Anna over to the floor to ceiling windows, into the light. The garden below was like an animated Monet, fluttering with the breeze, birds, and butterflies.

Aiden held her there, though he sensed her shyness. "There's no one out there; no one is looking, just me," he whispered. "Please, I want to see all of you."

Anna blushed deeply but did not move. Aiden's fingers glided tenderly from her face to neck to shoulders. Aiden's gaze held her breasts, and her nipples crinkled with anticipation. His fingers caressed unhurried, and as Anna's breathing became uneven as he placed his mouth over each nipple, sucking and tormenting her with his tongue. Anna raised her hands to touch Aiden, to ground herself in this electrical storm, but he gently pushed them back down to her sides. I'm not to move? Aiden shook his head slightly, tweaking her nipple between his teeth. Anna pressed her trembling fingers into her thighs and obeyed.

Aiden's hands drifted over her curves, his lips and tongue following the trail of goose bumps. Kneeling, while kissing her belly, his fingers followed the line of her rift between her cheeks, his hands dropped further to her inner thighs. A little pressure and Anna parted her legs until Aiden indicated to stop just as her nether lips parted with a sound like a small wet kiss.

Aiden dove in, lapping up her nectar, carefully avoiding her swollen nub. His tongue was impossibly long and skilled and was not at all shy or reluctant in its travels. His fingers if not stroking between her buttocks, were busy probing, drawing out every drop of moisture.

As he felt her muscles tighten and her breathing catch, he drew his tongue over her exposed nub, sucked it between his lips, and nibbled.

Anna cried out, her legs buckling and she dropped to her knees, shuddering. " Aiden," she struggled to breathe.

Aiden rose as Anna kneeled, body parts aligning perfectly, or so it seemed to Aiden. Anna looked up into his face and smiled. Her tongue peeked out and licked her lips and then gathered the pearl perched on Aiden's glistening head. Aiden resisted the painful urge to feel the back of her throat and he let Anna take control. He wasn't disappointed. Apparently, she was starving though maintained good manners. He loved that she listened to his thoughts and followed all of his suggestions. She finally silenced him by humming over his head and gently rolling his balls in her hand. Aiden stopped short of exploding and pulled Anna up off her knees to his bed. In one fluid motion, Anna was up in the middle of his ornate bed, legs open in an invitation. Aiden followed and aimed well, burying himself to the hilt and quickly began to conjugate Russian verbs. H yBepeH, BH HB-nneTecb, MM HB^neMcn... Anna heard Aiden's gravelly Russian accent in her mind, pushing her closer and closer to the edge. Aiden's thrusts were slow and, measured and perfectly placed.

"Please don't hold back anymore, Aiden" Anna pleaded breathlessly.

Aiden growled and let loose.

"Unnnghhh, yes, Aiden, Yes!"

"H coSuparocb gHnnoM.!"Aiden's accent was strained. "Fuck yes! Now, with me Anna!" As their bodies stilled and their breathing quieted, Anna and Aiden lay entwined basking in the glow of new found love.

Anna's thoughts drifted occasionally tickled by Aiden's. How can you be so like your sister yet so very different?

Reminded of Libby, Anna's thoughts became sour with guilt, and she wavered between loyalty to her sister and her undeniable bond with Aiden. I'm sorry Libby "We have to stop my sister, she's become obsessed..."

"Ian?" Aiden questioned.

"No. Not so much Ian as what he can give her. Immortality. She's planning to have him bite her tonight within the Stones."

Aiden was shaking his head "I don't think she can get Ian to give her that. He's not".

"No? Look at her path of destruction so far. She's very clever and a very, very talented um, a very talented witch."

"Kate? Did Libby..."

"It's a spell...I'm sorry, Aiden, I didn't know... I didn't think... I don't know where she's keeping the doll..."

"What? What doll?"

"It doesn't matter. We have to get Kate to Stonehenge, it'll break the spell."

THE END

OTHER BOOKS BY THE AUTHOR

Karmic Love

Undercover

Eternal Love

Undying Lust

The Good Taste

Offence and Justice

A Model for Murder

Lethal Legacy

Lethal Legacy 2

Paranormal Club

Enchanted Souls

Beginners of Nowhere

Wildflower

Mystic Agent

Dark Angel

Lonesome Moonlight

The Eerie Egg

A Romantic Crime .

Passionate Alien

Dragon Knight

The Critical Case

In the Shadow

Mental Asylum

Athena

Candy Spy

Hidden Veil